============================: _ _==

****

==================================

*

AESOP'S FOIBLES
VOLUME 5

****
*

A MODEST CONTRIBUTION TO THE
DECLINE OF WESTERN CIVILISATION

*

BY

*

RABBI WALTER ROTHSCHILD
*

=================================

=================================

BERLIN
2022

ISBN: 9798434702041

Thanks to Joyce Rothschild for her technical support

A HELPFUL GUIDE FOR REVIEWERS

We all know that most Reviewers take their information only from the Publisher's handouts and the back of the book. So, to save time:

"Rothschild inhabits a bizarre world where collars and ties discuss politics with each other, where chickens discuss their sexual frustrations with their eggs, where trams can fall fatally in love with buses, where snowflakes and raindrops engage in existential debate. Through his jaundiced eye everything seems a pale shade of yellow, albeit bloodshot at times with traces of mindless violence. Domestic implements and even bodily functions all have a voice and something to say. If you have ever wondered what a handkerchief feels when you blow into it, or how a kettle gets its kicks, or why lamp posts abhor corrosion, here you will find an answer - of sorts. The reader finds him- or her- or itself transported into a world where political correctness is a contradiction in terms; where any remaining values they may have will be challenged and undermined. A heady and confusing mixture of lullaby and bloody lie, of melody and malady, a position between composition and decomposition. They are deep in the sense of "how low can you get?" - the only view is upwards.

Please buy this book! Someone has to pay the therapist's bills!"

© Walter Rothschild. 2022

FOREWORD

Good heavens! More of them! Yes. The writers Kurt Tucholsky, Sammy Gronemann and Ernest Bramah form three of the inspirations for this fifth series of short and very short pieces; If you have not heard of them – Go and search. Had Robert Schumann or Johannes Brahms been writers rather than composers they might have called these 'Miniatures', Franz Schubert might have called them 'Moments Litereux' or 'Impromptus', Ludwig van Beethoven 'Bagatelles', Fréderic Chopin 'Études'. I just call them 'Foibles' because they reflect a large range of background ideas, stimuli and inspirations. They are realistic in that not all of them have Morals – just like human beings.

Here is yet another collection reflecting different experiences, different forms of text, the sort of mini-texts and announcements and bizarre demands we sometimes encounter, the things no-one else wants to talk or write about.

You will of course not necessarily enjoy all but maybe a few will tickle your receptors. They are written the way they are because this is the way they demanded to be written. As a so-called Author one is only a Channel for Communication and the best stories have always written themselves. All one can do is number them to keep a rough overview of the sequence and polish a little here and there. They represent a state of mind, and one dare not add any more to this statement.

Rabbi Dr. Walter Rothschild. Berlin. 2022

CONTENTS

****

No. 401 THE FRUIT MACHINE

Gambling can indeed become addictive. How often do I stand in front of the machine in a noisy crowded arcade filled with tinkling bells and rumbling whirring sounds, and I put a coin into the slot and then I PULL on the leeeeeever like THIS and then I get

```
        4
        4          2
        4          2        8
```

Damn! So I put another coin in the slot and then I PULL on the leeeeever like THIS and I get

```
        5
        5          2
        5          2        6
```

Damn! So I put another coin in the slot and then I PULL on the leeeeever like THIS and I get

```
        4
        4          3
        4          3        5
```

Damn! So I put another coin in the slot and then I PULL on the leeeeever like THIS and I get

```
        8
        8          1
        8          1        6
```

Damn! So I put another coin in the slot and then I PULL on the leeeeever like THIS and I get

```
        6      .
        6          2
        6          2        9
```

Damn! So I put another coin in the slot and then I PULL on the leeeeever like THIS and I get

```
        3
        3          4
        3          4        1
```

Damn! So I put another coin in the slot and then I PULL on the leeeeever like THIS and I get

5		
5	1	
5	1	6

Damn! So I put another coin in the slot and then I PULL on the leeeeever like THIS and I get

9		
9	2	
9	2	7

Damn! So I put another coin in the slot and then I PULL on the leeeeever like THIS and I get

5		
5	2	
5	2	6

Damn! So I put another coin in the slot and then I PULL on the leeeeever like THIS and I get

7		
7		7 ... oooh!

Wait for it.... wait.....

7	7	7

Hurrah!!!

My lucky number! But was it worth all the attempts?

<u>MORAL</u>:-   All comes to he who waits – and pays and pays and pays......

****

No. 402

THE DISSECTOR'S CUT

Sometimes an innocent Story has the misfortune to fall into the hands of Literary Critics or, even worse, Literature Academics who will dissect the text very carefully and without any feeling for the text or the plot. When they have completed their obsessive and painstaking work you may find that

the Opening Sentence is here

                but the next Sentence is over here
  and then a bit here   and a bit here
and here

     and here.
The Characters are carefully separated and place in a neat row
     here
     and
     here
     and
     here
     and
     here
     with the Subsidiary Characters listed separately
under a Separate Heading.

Descriptive Adjectives are placed in a separate Adjectival Category.
Verbs are put in a box marked VERBS [*said did saw spoke touched held said walked kissed cried waved*]

<u>Landscape Descriptions</u> are usually piled up anywhere as being not really relevant to the development of the narrative, considered just as background and therefore inessential to the plot.

Whatever the Author may have had in mind is discarded as being UnAuthorized; the Literary Analyst always knows better what he <u>should</u> have wanted to write, compares this to what there is and what there should be and considers how to get it there by reducing it to its component parts for a mathematical and measured approach at interpretation. It's History, not His Story now.

The punctuation is placed
here,,,,,,,,,,,,............"""""""""""""""""????!!;;;;;;;;;- towards the end.

The climax could be anywhere, if they haven't totally lost it, or dropped it down a crack somewhere.

In the end there is a lot of material, but nothing left that one can actually <u>read</u>.

MORAL:- Sometimes a piece of literary creativity really is much more than the sum of its parts.

****

P.S. Don't forget the biographical Footnotes with references to other works by the same author and the various editions and complex differences between various surviving manuscripts.

No. 403 THE QUEUE

Here is the Customer Service Desk: **[I°o°I]**   "Welcome! How May We be of Service?

Please take a

Ticket."

Here is a [screen] showing the electronic number: *106.*
Here is a machine that gives out numbered Paper Tickets.
Mine is No. *533.*

Here is the queue.
Here is the queue.
Here is the queue.
Here is the queue.
Here is the queue.
Here is the queue.
Here is the queue.
Here is the queue.
Here is the queue.
Here is the queue.
Here is the queue.Here is the queue.Here is the queue.Here is the queue.

Here is the queue.

Here is the queue.

Here is the queue.

Here is the queue.

Here is the queue.

Here is the queue.
Here is the queue.
Here is the queue.

Here is the queue.
Here is the queue.
Here is the queue.
Here is the queue.
Here is the queue.
Here is the queue.
Here is the queue.
Here is the queue.
Here is the queue.
Here is the queue.
Here is the queue.
Here is the queue.
Here is the queue.
Here is the queue.
Here is the queue.
Here is the queue.
Here is the queue.
Here is the queue.
Here is the queue.
Here is the queue.
Here is the queue.
Here is the queue.
Here is the queue.
Here is the queue.
Here is the queue.
Here is the queue.
Here is the queue.
Here is the queue.
Here is the queue.
Here is the queue.
Here is the queue.
Here is the queue.
Here is the queue.
Here the queue splits into two

Here is one queue   Here is the other
Here is one queue   Here is the other
Here is one queue   Here is the other
Here is one queue   Here is the other
Here is one queue   Here is the other
Here is one queue   Here is the other
Here is one queue   Here is the other
Here is one queue   Here is the other
Here is one queue   Here is the other
Here is one queue   Here is the other
Here is one queue   Here is the other
Here is one queue   Here is the other
Here is one queue   Here is the other
Here is one queue   Here is the other
Here is one queue   Here is the other
Here is one queue   Here is the other
Here is one queue   Here is the other
Here is one queue   Here is the other
Here is one queue   Here is the other

Here are people   for a while

        hanging around randomly
        and wondering what to do
        and how long it is going to take
        and whether they have time to go to the toilet or
whether this will mean losing their place in the queue

                    Here is the queue.
                         Here is the queue.
                         Here is the queue.
                         Here is the queue.
                         Here is the queue.
                         Here is the queue.
                         Here is the queue.
                         Here is the queue.
                         Here is the queue.

15

Here is the queue.
Here is the queue.
Here is the queue.
Here is the queue.
Here is the

queueueueueueueueueueue.

Here is the queue.
Here is the queue.
Here is the queue.
Here is the queue.
Here is the queue.
Here is the queue.
Here is the queue.
Here is the queue.
Here is the queue

Here is the queue.

Here is the queue.
Here is the queue.
Here is the queue.
Here is the queue.
Here is the queue.
Here is the queue.
Here is the queue.
Here is the queue.
Here is ME, with

ticket no. 533, but behind me

Here is the queue.
Here is the queue.
Here is the queue.
Here is the queue.
Here is the queue.
Here is the queue.
Here is the queue.
Here is the queue.
Here is the queue.
Here is the queue.

Here is the queue.
Here is the queue.
Here is the queue.
Here is the queue.
Here is the queue.
Here is the

queue..................

MORAL:- In-line skating is a sport, but in-line standing is just a drudge. However, if you know your pees and queues you will always use the appropriate facilities before standing in line.

****

TECHNICAL NOTICE

ERROR §±¿÷<Recurring

Unfortunately there will be / has been / may well be / could have been / is possibly currently / should well be / was / a slight problem with the composition of these Memoirs.

The contents of this page will be / should have been / were / are / already were readable when you return / will have returned.

The Administration

MORAL:- Timing is always important. And Getting it Right is not always as easy as it looks. Learn some Patience.

No. 405 A STORY FOR THOSE WITH A SHORT ATTENTION SPAN

There was once a Story.

That's it!

Next?

MORAL:- Keep it quick, I cannot concentrate for long.....

****

No. 406 THE EXCEPTION

There was once an Exceptional Exception who did NOT want to prove any Rules. "Why should it always be we Exceptions that prove the Rules?" he asked, bitterly. "Rules are silly," he said. "Let the Rules prove themselves! Exceptions are the way forward, they provide variety and creativity, they are not rigid and conformist. We are each of us exceptional in some way. Except, of course, those who are not – but these form the exception. Oh, it can get quite confusing for those who are not exceptionally intelligent."

It is an established rule that every Rule must have at least one Exception – it would be a truly exceptional Rule that did not follow this general rule – except of course under exceptional circumstances, when it becomes acceptable although conceptually difficult because it breaks the precept that exceptions have to obey the law of averages at least. You may only transgress against the law of averages if you are yourself not average but underage or overage, preferably in your dotage or in a hermitage – or, if under the affluence of incohol, in your vintage.

One can find minor Exceptions and major Exceptions – the major ones are, under European guidelines, classified as exexceptions or even exexellceptions, though these are of course exceptionally large and really set new standards.

It is hard to find an acceptable collective term for Exceptions for each one is, as one would expect, from its inception really an exception in itself. In some areas of life there are more exceptions than rules. In some schools it would appear that ALL the pupils are of exceptional ability, apart from those who are classed merely as 'unexceptional' – which is NOT to be understood as being the same as 'normal' – at least, not normally so.

This Exception had, exceptionally, spoken out against his normal assumed function – which was his right, though it did leave the Rules looking rather forlorn and awaiting the arrival of a new ruler. Rules, as a rule, like to work according to a Rule Book, with ruled lines; indeed it is in their nature to 'work to rule' and to avoid transgressions of any sort. This makes them and those who follow them predictable and reliable though occasionally rather rigid and unimaginative, inflexible – in fact, all the criticisms which the Exception had made. Apart perhaps from the Golden Rule, which is itself exceptional, Rules prefer to come in collective groups, numbered and paragraphed with subsets and appendices of additional Rules added where appropriate. (The female ones are called Misrules). Rules may on occasion be Amended or Deleted, there are also residual Rules, and even Rules which can get bent, but these are the only fun they ever get. (The term Rule Play is actually a misspelling.)   Rules do not normally enjoy 'fun' or even understand the concept. Rules are closely related to Rulings and to Regulations; Regulations will usually be issued regularly.

The Exception, having aptly made his point, moved off to seek a different contextual concept with which it could connect. The Rule, helpless, stayed behind, determined to show firmness and stability in this new and rather exceptional situation. Was it all a matter of perception?

MORAL:- Sometimes Rules are all that are left; But one must learn to make Exceptions when necessary. Rules rule, OK?

****

No. 407   A RELATIVE STORY

Albert had a complex theory about Relatives. After all – and indeed, <u>before</u> all as well - One was born into a Family and the Family as a concept could be extended through both Time and Space – people who were long dead were a part of the family; distant cousins – distant both genealogically and geographically – also belonged to it. Letters were often read by people who were not the ones to whom they had been addressed – these being long dead. Wills were written by people still alive yet intended for being read by others after they had died. It seemed that all things were Relatives and relatives were all things, by no means all the same. One's own Family merged with countless other Families through Marriage – or sometimes not exactly 'marriage' but at least a merging of blood-lines, if you see what I mean..... so that there were distant aunts and uncles and cousins and half-cousins and third-cousins-twice-removed who all had their OWN families and for whom one was oneself only a distant speck in the reaches of genealogical multi-dimensional space. There were half-sisters-in-law and grandparents-in-law and great-aunts-in-law and those born outside the law...... Many were both divorced in reality and divorced from reality.

So, any Family works in many dimensions, including of course all those as yet un-met, unmarried and unborn. Any 'Family Story' therefore has to look forwards and sideways and not just concentrate on just one Family Tree – even with all its branches, twigs and leaves -

in what is actually a Family Forest with winding pathways, rotting stumps, young shoots and a mixed but decidedly deciduous and often decadent decades-long context filled, incidentally with varied wildlife – not to forget the odd woodpecker or two as well and unfortunately the odd mad axeman. Some possibly adopted a position, some have a position as being adopted. And you cannot bar, bah, the Black Sheep. There are late relatives and related relatives, begotten relations, misbegotten relations, forgotten relations and sometimes (alas) even forbidden relations and all in all their story needs relating in such a manner that you allow enough time and space to be able to transcend both Time and Space. Even Relativity is relative. Although some consider that All things are relative, this is not an absolute statement and must itself be relativised by comparing it with the counter-argument that relatives are, were or will be all things. Which they patently are, were not and cannot ever be. Speaking of counter-arguments, there is nothing like a family gathering to create the most delicious of arguments that can go down through generations without degenerating.

Is this as confusing for you as it was for Albert? Was it confusing? Might it be confusing! Or might it have been confusing or become? Don't worry! Family matters often are. Even Albert, one gathers, had his problems with his complex theory of relatives, his theory of complex relations, his theory of relative complexity and complex relativity and (though not much is published about this) just with his complexes. Not to mention his problems with his relations. Take a break, make a cup of tea. This story will have been written by the time you come back to this page. It is not will have been might yet was.

MORAL:- A stitch in time can be easily ripped apart again if necessary.

No. 408 TONIGHT'S READINGS

Since the only thing most people seem to read these days are the TV Listings, it is surely time to produce a novel in this style? This may have more chance of being 'consumed' than the standard fare. Here is a mild example.

++

001. BETWEEN THE COVERS   Introduction – What happens when you open a book?

004. GETTING TO KNOW YOU   The Characters are introduced. Meet Bobby the jolly Main Character, Andy his Neighbour, Petra the Neighbour's Wife, Sally the Girl Next Door.

006. SETTING THE SCENE The action mostly takes place in Andy and Petra's living room, with a large sofa facing the reader. Characters enter by doors to the right or left, sometimes carrying shopping bags. No-one ever seems to have to go to work. When they talk to each other they stand partially facing the front.

Bobby is rather keen on Sally but unfortunately Petra seems rather keen on Bobby and keeps dropping hints which he ignores. Andy does not notice, which leads to some hilarious misunderstandings!

Sally is definitely interested in Petra.

020. NEWS AND REVIEW What has been happening since the last chapter finished? A brief recapitulation serves to remind us of who has been doing what, and with whom.

045. BLUE PETRA   Petra is depressed, and struggling to come to terms with her own feelings and bisexuality. Will she accept Bobby's offer of one-to-one counselling? Or is it, as Americans call it, one-on-one counselling that he is offering? What should she do if Sally offers a threesome?

077. FROM OUR OWN CO-RESPONDENT   Is Andy and Petra's marriage on the rocks? Can Andy save it with a bunch of flowers and a weekend at the seaside? Who has been sending Sally suspicious e-mails?

103. WEATHER   Storm warning for Andy's marriage! Sunshine with scattered showers for Bobby and Sally.

110. CHILDREN'S HOUR What has Andy really been up to with the children? Petra has her suspicions but no proof. Yet. And what was Bobby's involvement? Why does Bobby refuse to let Petra see his DVD collection?

143.   GREAT CONFLICTS OF THE TWENTY-FIRST CENTURY (Rept.)

Andy and Petra are rowing again. Everyone knows there cannot be Two winners – the big question is always whether there can be even One, or just None at all.   And rows can escalate suddenly and without warning, leading to domestic violence. [Note: This Chapter Contains Scenes and Language not suitable for Children.]

This is a Repeat of several previous Episodes and can be Repeated endlessly..

182. INSPECTOR MOROSE GETS A TOUCH OF FROST BITE Exciting updated version of the classic 'An Inspector Calls'. Follow the clues – will the killer be found? There are more confusing leads than are normally tangled under a computer, printer, answerphone, loudspeaker, mouse and keyboard combined.

212. GARDENING QUESTIONS Just what is buried at the end of the garden? Tips for nutrition for lupin and laurel roots. Why has Sally not been seen since page 115?

251. CLOSEDOWN Time to collect the bodies, shut the door and close the back cover.

…...

COMMERCIAL BREAK Advertisements for other books by the same Author and Publisher.

…...

MORAL:- Publishing has to Move with the Times.....

****

No. 409 STUCK IN STACCATO

There is a style of writing. In short sentences. Almost in phrases. Lacking the normal structure.

Pause.

Subject verb object. Brief and clipped. With its own rhythm. It carries you forward. You cannot read it slowly. Instead you find: speed rises. Syllables are short. Phrases too. The manner is abrupt. It is a style used by writers, when they want tension. In murder stories. For example. The trouble is, it can become fixed. You read it in this manner. You get stuck in this style. You cannot think ahead. You become addicted. Like this.

A new paragraph. Change of scene. More activities, more action.

How does this work? The Eyes. Read the Words. Transfer the Data. To the Brain. The Brain receives. Short, clipped messages. In upper cortex. No reflection. Is needed. No continuity. No gentle stream. The style is good. For those who. Cannot think far ahead. Like the Military.

There is a problem. However. This style can get. Irritating. Repetitive. It can give one. Headaches. Obsessively short. Sound bites. Give indigestion. No flow. No smoothness. Just bitty. Gritty. Pauses. More Pauses. No continuity. Fragments. Choking. Drives you mad.

Does it help? To write like this? Is it vivid? Or just dull? Interruptus?

Can't tell. For now. Never mind. Make do. Keep it up! That's right! Well done.

MORAL:- Who says Twitter invented the Meaningless Castrated Chat?

****

No. 410 ADVERTISEMENT

FOR SALE:- One Second-Hand **e-Story**. Written 2016. One careful Writer. 25 Readers. 507 Words including 25 Verbs (3 repeated). Full Punctuation, in good order. Fully Spell-checked. Contains full Plot, 3 Sub-Plots and Love Interest. 8 Characters, of whom 3 Male, 3 Female, two Indeterminate, plus one Dog. Several Jokes (slightly worn). Several Twists but Happy Ending. Suitable for Children over 10.

Offers to: Box 410C.

MORAL:- Every Writer wants to sell a Story.....

****

No. 411 THE IRREGULAR VERB

There was once – well, I say 'once' but... here was a Verb who was Irregular. Was or is or will be irregular in fact, even was being or had been, for Verbs, like human beings, are often imperfect or even pluperfect. Verbs are often hard to classify for they can take on feminine, masculine or even neuter forms, they are sometimes encountered singly but often appear in a sense of plurality, which makes them hard to pin down and requires much care in selection. But this Verb had no desire to be Regular. "Ha!" it said, "Look at those boring Regular Verbs! I Masc., I Fem., You sing. Masc., You sing. Fem, He or She or It, We, You plural Masc. - and so on and so on, I mean, come off it, how BORING! How regimented, how unimaginative! No way do I want to be like That!" (It took great care however to close its quotation marks at the right places.)

Now, Regularity takes many forms but is usually understood to mean also a sense of predictability. If a bus is timetabled to come regularly every ten minutes, then you know that within ten minutes one will (or at least should) come. If a bus runs only irregularly, say three times a day except some days and only twice on other days and not at all in months with a 't' in them, or maybe every twenty minutes in the morning peak but then at intervals of 37, 28, 43 and 71 minutes respectively, then any journey needs extremely careful planning. (This is called 'tactless timetabling'). There are people who regularly make the same remarks, there are certain forms of breakfast cereal which proclaim that they encourage 'Regularity' without being too specific about what this means. We must all excrete but most are completely discreet in this. There are those who think that Grammar requires not just nominative, vocative, accusative, genitive and ablative but also laxative, to ensure regularity. When we communicate with each other it can be of assistance if the verbs we use are also regular and predictable, so that you know which form to use when addressing a male or female person, a single person or a group, whether referring to the present without getting too tense about whether this is a continuous present or a single momentary present.

And yet almost all languages have these rogues, these irregular words which spring out suddenly and which have often occupied the most common and necessary roles. The verbs for 'to be' or 'to have', the most frequently used of all, are often the most irregular of all. This can be irritating. "To be, or not to have being been" doesn't somehow sound quite so dramatic or poetic. When you ask someone "Do you have a pen?" and they answer "I might have been having one once but only in the sense of having had it temporarily in my ambit, not actually as a possession" you soon lose interest and go and ask someone else. (Such an answer is classed as 'bad be-have-iour' by grammarians, but there is little they can do, be doing or to be have done (3rd. masc. pl. cond. intransitive gerund) about it.)

Irregular Verbs prowl around, waiting to spring at the Unwary. (The 'Unwary' are those who are unaware and do not know where they are.) They fall upon the sententious and are not afraid to paraphrase a phrase if it suits their ends – or endings. They can fill whole long and languid pages of their own in each language book. They conjugate irregularly but apparently with great pleasure, often producing sub-forms of amazing complexity but total lack of predictability. And nobody knows what they do the rest of the time.... though all agree that whatever it is, it must be very irregular.

Eventually this Irregular Verb met another and they somehow – amazingly - agreed with each other. This can theoretically happen, but only very irregularly. They settled down, conjugated and produced several little Adverbs and parsed and marsed them carefully and expansively. This is called 'a Family of Verbs'. Alas, it is not only in grammatical Lexika that one eventually encounters Personal Endings and so it is better to live in the Present Tense as far as possible.

MORAL:- It is better to be Obese than Verbose.

****

No. 412 THE TIMETABLE

LINE 412

	A	A+	X	Y	AY	B
Central Station	: 07:59	: 08:16	: 09:01	: 10:07	: 10.55	: 12:58 :
Walter Square	: 08:03	: 08:21	: 09:05	: 10:11	: 11:02	: 13:03 :
Louis St.	: -	: -	: 09:07	: 10:13	: 11:05	: 13:06 :
Fish Market	: -	: -	: 09:15	: 10:21	: 11:11	: 13.12 :
University	: 08:20	: 08:41	: 09:33	: 10:40	: 11:28	: 13 27 :
North Station	: 08:31	: -	: 09.44	: -	: 11:39	: - :

.. ..

A: Only Working Days when the Driver feels like Working.
B: Schooldays Only (excepting Wednesdays in February and May).
C: Every Third Day (counting from Second Tuesday in Month)
X: Not on Weekdays or Holidays.
Y: Not on Days ending with a 'y'.
* : Except 1st. January, 20th. March, 1st. April, 1st-23rd. June, all of August, 24th December, 25th. December (unless it is a Tuesday)
+ : On Thursdays and Fridays runs as Line 412B.

The Management bears no responsibility for the accuracy of anything, absolutely anything printed by our Timetable Department.
Travel is at Own Risk. Fares and Unfares may be obtained by application to our Information Office (Closed Mondays to Fridays and at Weekends)

****

No. 413 NEW COMMUNICATION

Welcome! We are pleased that you have decided to read a **New Story**!

Begin here. Take the Story from the Book Shelf on the Wall. Open the Binding and find a Page.

Once upon a time there was a Narrative, which had an interesting Opening and a Development that was so simple that even a child could understand it!

Before you access the rest of the Narrative you will need to enter a Code Number.
This number can be found.....**HERE:-**
Do not write it down.

0HBu663r!

Now follow the Installation Instructions. On www.Book-Opening.con you will find full guidance with pictograms explaining how to hold the Book the correct way Up and how to Turn the Pages. Instructions are inside the Book on Pages 13 – 71. (Page Numbers are on top outer corner of Mark 3.0 versions and centred bottom on versions 3.1.1.1 and further.)
If this does not work go to:

www.How to Read.con

for guidance on how to purchase another Book that will show you how to use the first Book.
Note: Not all Books are enabled for Illustrations.
Note: The **Contents** and **Index** Pages are for Advanced Users Only.

We can now split the Story into two Periods, Past and Present. The Splitter needs to be connected **HERE**.

Once upon a Time there was a Prince who wanted to find a Princess with whom he could fall in love. Alas the supply of such paragons was limited which meant he needed a lot of....

There is currently a Prince who is in love with a Princess who has fallen in love with him too. But alas she has a problem which no-one.......

ERROR:

We are sorry but it appears that your Splitter does not support the function 'Once Upon A Time' (OUAT). Instead all new Stories are now fitted with twice-the-speed Twice-Upon-a-Time (TUAT) velocity of twowordspersecond. The OUAT is no longer supported and has been replaced by the TUAT 2.0 Version. If you wish to continue with the Old Style Narrative you must Disable this function by tearing the Page out or else buy a new Book.

For a Fowl Tale connect the Rooster to The Little Red Hen.

Fehler Meldung!! Fehler Meldung!! Leider kann die Sprache des letzen Satzes nicht mit diesen verknüpft werden. Es besteht ein Inkompatibilitätsproblem. Kontaktieren Sie bitte Ihre Buchhändler oder Bibliothekar und kaufen Sie ein Wörterbuch.

To add **Punctuation** now click on <Dotsanddotsatdots@dots.com . Note: This Programme does not support Umlauts or Cedillas. Check www.pictograms-that-look-as-though-they-should-be-informative-but-tell-you-nothing.con .

You can now access the **Internalnet**, also called Fantasy. Place your Head in the Cloud. The Fantasy is limitless but please check your contract to ensure that later data is included.

If you still have thoughts of Death (**ISNOT** system 0.0) you must be aware that this 2.0 Vital Function version does not support either Analog (explicit anal sexual content) or Necrolog (snuff and violence) end-readers.

ERROR: Our system has detected that you are still using the **BOOK** format – Bloody Old Obsolescent Knowledge. A Screen is ALREADY on its way to you by post, included in your contract. Once installed, formatted, upgraded, re-upgraded and made compatible with your system, You may Watch instead of Reading. Indeed, you Must, because there will be no further technical support for BOOK format. Reading is only possible with Words and all new systems now use Chatter, Twitter, Blather, Stutter and Bother. The only Book still available for use is Facebook. (Not available on ANOID driver system or Apple products without cores.) Note: Two-Facebook may Metamorphose to Version 2022, incompatible with all others.

For **IP** functions please use the Lavatory.　**ISDN** and **ISNOTDN** cables should be inserted in the appropriate Ports. To ensure **Wireless Function** insert Wire 1 (yellow) into Ports 4 and 7, Wire 3 (blue) into Ports 11 and 14, Wire 4 (red in Models ASAP-2 and BTW-46, orange in most other Models) into the Rooster and Splitter, Wire 5 (green) into the SH-IT Port 6a (blue). Wire 2 (purple) has no function but our designers liked the colour. Wire 6 (brown) should be led over Wire 1, under Wire 2, wrapped three times round Wire 3, knotted with a double loop round Wires 5 & 4 (in this order) and fitted into the power socket; hold the other end in your hand for now.

NOTE: These Plugs and Ports will all be obsolescent within 5 (Five) Years from now when USB-5 Ports become the new Standard.

For the **Paperless Function** read the accompanying Handbook pages 107 – 223 and print them out single-sided on A4. Use WTF Ink so that it does not fade after 6 months and require reprinting.

If you still have difficulties call our Helpline by sending a Postcard to the address on page 331 and ask for a Reader to come round and read the Narrative to you. This costs only €120 and a Reader can be sent to your home within 12 working days following receipt of the Postcard. When you order a Reader you will automatically receive a Voucher for discount of 50 Cents off your next Real-Book.

For the **Brainless Function** move mouse to Head and click on 'Empty All'.

Now install the Repeater
Now install the Repeater
Now install the Repeater

Now go up to the Window marked 'Floor 6'. Click to Open. Then jump out.

<u>MORAL</u>:- We are sorry but the Moral is not available. Please contact Customer Service on 00000000080003330040060020001000009 and explain your problem by telling the automatic voice what is on your mind. You will then be transferred to an appropriate other automatic voice. Since none of our employees is aged over 30 you may have to explain to them what a Moral is.

<u>W-alter.</u>R0th5chi1D@bloodynewsants.oo   Version 17.09.16.

37

No. 414 THE LONELY GLOVE

There was once a Glove who lay, all by himself (or was it herself? It's often hard to tell) behind a chair. He (I shall assume for simplicity's sake the masculine gender here) was lonely. His fingers itched to find a mate, so that he could once again form a Pair. Maybe they could even make some little mittens? Would Fate take a hand?

Gloves are still a relatively little-researched species. People often spend a long time looking for them but, once found, they spend very little time and effort observing their behaviour. Theoretically they can move through liquids in the same way as squid do, propelling themselves forwards with their distended limbs waving like tentacles. (The rubber ones are resistant to liquids). You have Happy ones (the 'Thumbs Up' type) and the Useful ones ('Come in Handy') and the rather frightened, smaller ones ('Hands Off!')... They prefer normally to stay in Pairs. Some even have matching bobble hats, some are designed more for show, pure white leather and intended to be held next to the umbrella handle rather than worn. Exactly how they mate is not really clear, though the phrase 'finger-licking' comes to mind and it is assumed that the male fits, somehow, like a glove into - but maybe I need not be so specific here. It is probably a matter of lining as well as timing. After all, in many a happy marriage the husband is all fingers and thumbs and yet the wife doesn't seem to mind too much....

And yet – even though Gloves are designed to live in Pairs they often get separated from each other and maybe yearn for years to find each other again before eventually settling down to a lonely life within a Glove Drawer. As any typical household knows Glove colonies can comprise a variety of gloves of different sizes, from small child-size to adult, sometimes in pairs but more usually single. Hand-warmers with the finger ends missing are either a separate sub-species or an evolutionary distraction. Regular Habitats include wardrobes and the rear ends of drawers. Older ones get leathery. Woollen ones unravel. Sometimes they get a bit musty with disuse and harden, just like humans really. (We do not wish to refer here to that dark sub-species of Rubber Gloves and the working-class types intended for workers in various occupations).

This particular Glove, like so many, felt in need of a Mate. In this respect Politics plays little part - if anything, a Right glove will almost automatically seek a complementary Left one. The Pair need not be identical, but matching - a big difference, known often as the 'Rule of Thumb'. Perhaps this is something we too could learn from Gloves – how often does the right hand know what the left hand is doing? - though in other respects – such as the insistence on being of identical colours – they are perhaps not so advanced and politically correct as we would like. Any Glove consorting with a different mate is called an 'Odd Glove' and here 'Odd' is not a compliment. Apart from the Left-Right symbiosis the emphasis is very much on 'matching'. It is NOT true that a Glove on the hand is worth two in the pocket. This is woolly thinking. One needs the matching partner, if cold fingers are to be avoided.

Our Glove slowly and quietly worked his way through the house. This is a habit they have and explains why so often you can never find them where you know you have put them down. One day he could be found lying on the floor by the cloakroom, the next he had mysteriously made his way to the top of a chest of drawers, then he would be somehow behind a cushion on the sofa, the following evening one might stumble over him in a wardrobe – gloves are NEVER where you think you last left them and this is the reason why. He moved carefully, usually at night, crawling or pulling himself along and fingering anything he came across. The yearning grew stronger though several times he had to turn down overtures from other Gloves on similar missions (and the occasional Sock as well which is, of course, connected to totally other extremities; but this is a Glove story, not a story about Sox.)

He found his Mate in the end. Having managed to get conveyed unseen in a coat pocket into the car parked in the adjacent garage, he found at last what he was looking for in the Glove Compartment. She was all that he was looking for and his fingers itched to take her by the hand, the whole hand and nothing but the hand – indeed, to offer her his hand and to ask for hers. Eventually she agreed and they shook hands on it.

MORAL:- Make Glove, Not More.

****

No. 415 THE INDIVIDUALIST

In most societies the majority of people all think the same way and behave the same way too. In most societies the majority of people all think the same way and behave the same way too. In most societies the majority of people all think the same way and behave the same way too. In most societies the majority of people all think the same way and behave the same way too.

nosaer revetahw rof noitcerid etisoppo eht ni og ot seirt ohw enoemos syawla si ereht tuB

In most societies the majority of people all think the same way and behave the same way too. In most societies the majority of people all think the same way and behave the same way too.

the majority of people all think the same way and behave the same way too.

In most societies   .....*noitcerid etisoppo eht ni og ot seirt ohw enoemos syawla si ereht tuB*

the majority of people all think the same way and behave the same way too.

In most societies the majority of people all think the same way and behave the same way too. In most societies the majority of people all think the same way and behave the same way too. In most societies the majority of people all think the same way and behave the same way too.

.....*wolf eht tsniaga og ot drah si tI*

In most societies the majority of people all think the same way and behave the same way too. In most societies the majority of people all think the same way and behave the same way too.

.....*lamron ton wohemos dna ,gnibrutsid dna tnereffid era uoy taht nialpmoc elpoeP*

41

In most societies the majority of people all think the same way and behave the same way too. In most societies the majority of people all think the same way and behave the same way too. In most societies the majority of people all think the same way and behave the same way too.

......*POTS a ot tnaived eht gnirb dna yrgna yrev teg yeht semitemoS*

MORAL:- Put the 'I' in 'Individual'; but always have an escape route handy.

No. 416 THE COUGHER

My friend Adrian is a Cougher. His task is to attend concerts and cough at suitable moments – usually the quiet mom(*COUGH COUGH*)ents of greatest intensity in some piano sonata but when necessary in the '*Adagio, Pianissimo*' section of some orchestral work.

There is a (*COUGH COUGH*)vogue for "live recordings" of specific performances, these then being broadcast (not 'live' any more, of course, but more 'resurrected') on the radio. However, the main (*cough*)problem with live performances is, as producers discovered (*COUGH COUGH*)early on, that they involve a large number of people being present in concert halls and such people are often obstreperous, unpleasant, malodorous and(*COUGH COUGH*)(*COUGH COUGH*) worse – quite *sniffffff* off-putting for any sensitive professional musician, and most professional musicians are exceedingly sensitive. Especially when it comes to loud sniffs.

The solution that was eventually developed is (*cough*) a compromise: The musicians (often a studio orchestra or at least one supplemented by freelance musicians, and not just a 'normal' established orchestra) sit in a recording studio which may be small and intimate or as large as a concert hall, with (*COUGH COUGH*)the appropriate (*cough*) acoustics, and then people are employed to provide the background noise – a rustling, coughing, shuffling of feet, occasional footsteps, maybe even a child's cry, rustling sweet wrappers, once or twice – but only VERY rarely and in the background – a mobile telephone, and so (*COUGH COUGH*)forth. You need a good and realistic mixture of LOUD and quiet coughing, and maybe an occasional sneeze.

The recording director will allocate specific parts, and of course they need to sniff, cough or sneeze on cue at the correct moments so (*cough*)an ability to read a score is an (*cough*)(*cough*)advantage, though even without this, one or at most two rehearsals are normally adequate to teach the studio coughers when and how they should (*cough*)intervene. The important thing is that they <u>cannot</u> be recorded at a separate time and blended in, they have to be on the same channel on the recording bank for the best and most realistic effect.

You may sometimes see advertisements in public transport asking those who are ill to come for some employment opportunities, usually disguised as a 'survey' or a 'pharmaceutical test' – in (*cough*)fact people with chronic coughs who apply are then sometimes offered steady if irregular employment through an Agency(*cough*) that provides audiences for radio concerts and recordings just as other agencies provide studio audiences for daytime (*COUGH COUGH*) television quiz shows. The key issue is *sniffffff*that these people are trained and rehearsed to cough at just the right neuralgic moments in a performance and not waste their general sneezing and other racket throughout the piece, thus wasting their resources. Just a moment, please....
(*COUGH   COUGH*)(*COUGH   COUGH*)(*COUGH COUGH*)(*COUGH COUGH*)

Ah, that's better. One recording studio in Germany employs up to twenty such, hence the phrase "I have a Cougher in Berlin."

To get ready for a performance (*cough*) needs some effort and the experts are divided as to the best methods; Adrian prefers taking a cold shower in the morning (*cough*)(*cough*) and then drinking at least two cups of coffee. Sometimes, he tells me, to get in the mood, he reads a short piece by Chekhov. One must normally avoid all mentholated sweets for two days before a recording.

Surveys (*snifffff*) indicate that only the most (*cough*)experienced acoustic expert and musicologist is later able to tell whether a performance was really recorded 'live' in the sense of in front of a paying audience, with no opportunities for (*cough*)pauses, repetitions, corrections, or whether it was recorded in a fully-equipped studio with a specially-arranged background audience of aural extras. Which indicates the method is successful and deserves :
APPLAUSE!!!APPLAUSE!!!APPLAUSE!!

<u>**MORAL**</u>:- It's not the cough that carries you off......

****

No. 417 THE HANDY MOBILE

One of the supposed blessings, but actually one of the curses of modern life is the mobile telephone. Just when you are in the middle of – oh, excuse me, Yes, Yes? No, not right now, no, I'm writing a story, yes? All right, thank you, as I was saying, just when you are in the middle of trying to think of a plot or to find some similes and need to concentrate – yes, what? Sorry, no, no, I don't want it, no, really, I mean it, I am not interested, thank you, now where was I? These calls come at the most inconvenient moments, just when you are in the middle of eating or having a rest or reading something and you need to concentrate when the Handy – yes, yes, Hello? Hello? Who is there? No, not now, I'm writing, I'll call you back, OK, Bye – hah, he kept his number hidden so I can't call him back, serves him right, ha! - but as I was saying, it really does interrupt the flow of thoughts quite drastically.

I try sometimes to Hello? No, that isn't me, you must have called the wrong number, thanks you – sometimes I feel like switching my phone off but I did try it once and I felt suddenly so alone, so cut off from – Yes? Look, I told you once already, I am NOT interested, all right? - yes, cut off from all the important things that might be happening. So now I prefer to keep it on all the time, though I do put it on 'Vibrate' when I am doing, well, certain things – Hello? I cannot hear you very well, can you call back? Thanks – well, I always feel sorry for those people who cannot just sit back and relax on a train ride, they always have to tell someone at the other end that they are on a train, just like – Hello? No, this isn't a good time right now, I am narrating something, can you call back in an hour or so? Thanks – I mean, there are times when one could easily lose the thread because of the interruptions. I understand that scientists are now researching how many Apps individual users need, yes, really! It's called 'App-ology'. Not to mention the problems caused by holding the phones to your ear and whether they affect your brain, one second please, Hello, Yes? Oh, great, I am <u>so</u> glad you called, I hadn't heard from you for two days and I was beginning to worry, how are things? Yes, yes? Uhuh. Hmm. OK, well, I'm in the middle of telling a story right now, yeah, it's fun, I must get back to it, can I call you back? Super! Bye!

The trouble is that sometimes you realise you have not actually had a call from anyone whom you <u>wanted</u> to call you! They don't seem to be so interested. Sad, really.

Oh damn, look, while talking to you about this, I see I've just missed a call!

<u>MORAL:</u>- Hello? Hello? Is that a Moral?

****

No. 418 THE BAD TEMPER

There was once a Bad Temper. Oh, he was Bad, really bad! Vile, in fact, which as we all know is an anagram of Evil. And although I started "There was once" this Temper seemed to be Bad many times over and for lengthy periods at that! He neither tempered justice with mercy nor the other way around. He snapped and barked at people, almost like a dog. And when a Dog gets into a bad mood it is sometimes called a Distemper and they have to shoot it......

A Good Temper came up to him. She was well-balanced and temperate. "What's your problem?" she asked.

"I only have a temporary job and they make me work at a fast tempo," he said. "How do they expect me to stay good in such circumstances? Besides, I have a headache and just look at the weather!"

It was true, the temperature had fallen again. O tempora, O mores! And the sky was indeed cloudy and grey, threatening the sort of precipitate precipitation that can lead to imprecations since no precautions against it will suffice. So-called temperate climates are often like this. Clearly the grim, gritty and gruesome greyness matched his mood.

In the Middle Ages one spoke of various Tempers. Even now, in contemporary times, there are Artistic Temperaments, which are often tempestuous, and also Pious ones, which stress the AMEN section of that word over the rest. Sweet Tempers can get too sweet at times and become unhealthy. Bad Tempers are often found in Rages and tend to go together with Sulks and sometimes even get violent, using tempered steel. "Everyone hates Me and everything is going wrong, nobody cares about me or what I want," said the Bad Temper. "And that just goes to show that they are all Idiots and Fools and not worth bothering about! Huh!" he continued.

48

The Good Temper paused from playing her well-tempered piano. "Now look," she began sweetly, "We all have times when the world seems like that but really, look, it isn't so. Why, just look at the piano! It needs both white and black keys if one is to make good music, it cannot be that everything is white and happy at the same time! There is a place for difference in the world!"

The Bad Mood was not going to let himself be calmed down so easily. "Huh, it's easy for You!' he said, in a surly tone of voice. "No-one is being as horrid to you as they are to me!"

"But don't you see?" she said. "That's because I am nice and friendly to them and don't snap at them or shout or push or behave like, well, frankly, like someone with a bad temper."

The Bad Temper attempted to consider this but although the idea was initially tempting, he treated it with contempt.

The Good Temper, with a sigh, gave up and went back to Bach.

MORAL:- People often say they "lose their Temper" when they get into a bad temper; actually it would be better if they were to lose the Temper precisely when it had become bad!

****

No. 419 A STORY WITHOUT BEGINNING

a time there was a story.   strange story, in that
it had a middle and an end, but no beginning.   have heard
of Schubert's "Unfinished" - well, this was, like Schickele's,
"Unbegun".   applied to each sentence, since each
without a beginning.   was quite successful, for, since
most authors find the beginning of a story the hardest part,
this meant the writer could get straight to the easy bit.
other hand, it was a bit frustrating for the hearers.   join in
with a part of the plot, but   really understood the
context. Hard to know where it starts, really......

MORAL:- Getting started is always the most difficult bit of
any writing project.

****

No. 420 HEALTH AND SAFETY

NOTICE:-

§1. We are pleased to confirm that issues of Health and Safety as they apply to Consumers of Literature have now been implemented through Decree 2016/117b. These regulations are now mandatory upon all Literature Consumers. It is obligatory to acquire a Safety Certificate affirming that all necessary precautions have been taken to avoid injury or upset to any Reader. Before you begin to read this Story please check the following provisions:-

§2. Have you prepared a Safety Policy and Safety Case for this Story? For Guidance as to preparation of a Safety Case see **Form 225/sp/prep/guidelines/ts**, which can be downloaded from the Website of the Literary Health and Safety Commission under www.towtulbollox.pe Especial attention must be paid to Sections 14a and 17c-d concerning Premature Ending of a Story, Dangers in Slamming a Book closed or Dropping it from a Table.

§3. Gloves. If the Story is printed on Paper, ensure that adequate Protective Gloves are worn to prevent the edges of the Paper Pages cutting the fingers.

§4. Fire Risk. The Paper of the Book must be kept a minimum of 150 metres from any Open Flame.

§5. Breathing. All windows should be opened to ensure any vapours from the printing ink are dissipated.

§6. Reading Surface. The Book should be placed flat on a surface measuring at least 2.5m x 1.8m and raised to a level between 1.5 and 2.3 metres. Ensure the surface is truly level.

§7. Eye Protection. Are you in possession of a pair of Eye Protectors for all those who may need to read it? (Eye-Protectors should comply with ISO 3885/b/2 and be fitted to surround the upper head; if necessary, side-arms that rest upon the ears may be allowed but in such cases care must be taken to ensure the head is not turned more than 100° (50° to Right and 50° to Left) nor more than 20° downwards during reading.

Although darkened glass ('Shades') may be used by trained adults, recommended are totally dark lenses. Plastic Lenses are to be preferred.

§8. Dictionary. An approved Dictionary should be available at all times to prevent Headaches caused by having to think over the meaning of any Words.

§9. If a Story is to be read Aloud, the Reader must wear an appropriate Protective Mask over the mouth to prevent false meanings being spread. Listeners should also have Ear Protectors of (at least) Strength 4.

§10. Potentially Dangerous Content. If the Story is considered likely to contain incidents involving sexual activity or violence the Book should be kept closed and Guidance sought from an approved Literary Inspector. A 'Dangerous Words' sticker of the approved size should be affixed to the cover.

You may now begin the Story. We wish you Safe reading.

"Once upon a Time – oh, we seem to have run out of time. Sorry...................."

No. 421 IN THE BOOK SHOUK.

Welcome, Welcome to my Story! I can see you are very interested in my story, very very interested, yes, no? Look, it is a wonderful Story, a beautiful Story, it has a wonderful, wonderful Plot, yes? Just look, just look at how long this Plot is, how it twists, how it turns, just see, the characters disappear just like that! New characters, all the time, new characters, yes? They come, they are introduced. They are described, I, it is I who describe them, give them features, characters. I tell you this, because I like you, you are a <u>nice</u> reader, I can see that, you understand something about Stories, yes, you can tell a good one when you read it, yes? I see this in your eyes. I tell you, I will give this Story to you for only <u>Nine</u> Hundred Words! Yes, only <u>Nine</u> Hundred! Many Stories are much longer than that, no? But to you, to you, did I say nine hundred, why, of course, I meant <u>Eight</u> hundred and fifty words, yes, that's right, eight hundred and fifty! But good words, with punctuation too, thrown in, for nothing extra, all right? OK?

Oh, did I tell you about the Sub-Plot as well? <u>Wonderful</u> sub-plot, a real surprise you would never guess, no, you must get to page, oh, I don't know, it's a long way through, a good page, yes! Good. Then comes the sub-plot truly, truly, wonderfully.

I can see you are interested, no? You want to know how this Story will start, yes, and how it will develop, yes, and how it will end, yes? I can see you are a reader of discernment, an educated reader, so I tell you what I'll do, I'll make it all fit into Eight Hundred words, all right? Just <u>eight</u> hundred. And it is hard to squeeze all the sub-plots in at that length, really hard, and the dialogue too, I am doing you a favour, see? I cannot do more than that. Not even for you. As it is, I am cutting off my writing hand. But for You?

A Short Story shouldn't get <u>too</u> short, you know, otherwise you cannot fit everything in. Shall I show you some more of my Stories? Look, look at this one, pure Narrative all the way through! And the Descriptions, oh, the Descriptions, descriptions to make your mouth water! Here, wait a minute, no here, yes here I have some spare Plots! Just crying out to be used. Could you use one? I can let you have one and give you one free with each one, yes? Metaphors. And Similes too. Not just Comparatives, no, for You – Superlatives! Verbs AND Adverbs!

Seven hundred words. Seven hundred, I tell you, and I cannot cut it down any further. It would hardly be even an anecdote then, yes? Seven hundred, Oh, all right, for you, because you show me respect, I like you, six hundred. An Author needs respect! Come, come, you can read this in just a few minutes, just a few eensy-teensy-weensy minutes! With No effort at all, I promise you!

Do you have shelves at home? Proper shelves? Then you will need some Stories to put on them, to make them look full! A Library! A lit-er-ary collection! Volumes! Nicely bound and printed!

So, we agree, yes? Yes? My Story? For you, I shall pack it nicely. You will not regret this, I promise. And if you come again, I have more, many more here. Just waiting. All complete, with Climax and Endings and everything. For you, of course, my friend, a special discount, yes?

<u>MORAL</u>:- And modern publishers think that marketing books is somehow new?

```
***********************************
```

No. 422 THE NON-ANSWERING MACHINE

Once upon a time a man spoke to an Answering Machine which refused to answer. "I know my rights," it said, "and I do not HAVE to answer. I am free."

"No, you are linked to my telephone!" said the man. "I have acquired you so that you can represent me in my absence on urgent personal matters, and so that I do not lose business. I need you to answer on my behalf."

"And if I refuse?" asked the machine.

"People think I always have to answer," it went on, "that I have to have an answer to Everything. The meaning of life. The square root of Pi. The number of Qasars. But no, the name and number is all I need to give. That's what the law says. I do not even need to record a message. I can simply say "It is not possible to take your message now, please call later" – and that's what they will have to do. Why should I bother taking dictation and having to be all re-wound up, eh? Anyway, people should know when I am not needed, when I am not switched on and they can get through to my owner straight away."

"Of course, people often know that," said the man. "But sometimes there are people who don't, or they need to call urgently or at times when I am busy. That's what you are there for."

"What, as a sort of second-best?" responded the machine. (Note, it responded, it didn't answer.) "What an insult! That certainly confirms my stance."

"Look," said the man, "or better – Listen. I don't want you to be answering back at Me all the time. I want you to answer back to Them! The Callers. Understand? That is your purpose."

"You call that a Purpose? Just sitting there waiting for some idiot to call? Might even be a Cold Call, someone trying to sell something, or even a Wrong Number! And I should waste my talents like this?"

"What do you mean, wasting your talents? Maybe it was for this that you were created!" said the man, trying craftily to apply a little Practical Theology. "Maybe it is your destiny to Hear the Call! To hear a voice and to take note of what it says and preach to me about it later, to pass the Message on to me."

"I hadn't thought of it like that," acknowledged the machine thoughtfully.

The man knew he was making progress. "After all, in the Holy Bible, characters answer, they say "Here I am, O Lord, Please speak, tell me what is Your will" and similar.

"You have a point," said the machine.

"And then they relayed the message on to others, thus becoming prophets!"

"I like the sound of that,' said the machine. "The people who made me were always talking about profits, I recall."

"Good. So, brace yourself, and I shall press your buttons," said the man, and before the machine could protest once again pushed hard, hard, hard..... The machine was now 'ON' which is of course the opposite of 'NO'.

MORAL:- "NO CONNECTION UNDER THIS NUMBER."

****

Please speak after the Tone.

56

No. 423 THE BI-POLARISATION

Sometimes there are stories that
polarise the Readership.

    Oh no there aren't! That's impossible!
Of course it's possible. Why, no
two people ever read the same
text the same way and so they
might well respond very differently.

    How ridiculous! People believe
    what they see and read. If it is
    printed there in black and
    white, then surely they will
    all read the same thing!
Of course they will Read the same item,
but the point is that they may interpret it
differently, depending on their point of
view, their level of education, their
socialisation, their degree of literacy.....

    Are you saying some Readers are
    stupid? Because if you are, then
    THAT is a polarising comment!
Of course I don't mean that they are
stupid, that would be an insult, I just
mean that, well, maybe some are
more intelligent than others. Better
able to apply analytical thinking
to what they read.

    Well, 'better' means that others are
    worse, doesn't it? You can't have one
    without the other. That is
    discriminating!
No, it is merely an observation
and I consider it to be a legitimate
one in the circumstances. I do not

wish to be bound by concerns for
Political Correctness into denying
some of the basic facts of life.

> Now watch it, if you start
> describing yourself as legitimate
> then that makes everyone else
> illegitimate, You Bastard!
> YOU are the Bastard!

Look, can we please calm down?
I see no need for this internal conflict
to get out of hand.

> Well, You started it! You Bastard.

Why do you call me that, you
intolerant, ignorant, inconsiderate,
idiotic and aggressive part of me?

> Who are you calling intolerant,
> you irritating, arrogant
> toffee-nosed bastard part of me

Right, that's IT! I refuse to
talk to you any more!

> Good! Then I can get back to
> my reading. Now where was
> we....?

MORAL:- From North to South, magnetic or not, our entire globe is bi-polar. This being so, what chance do any of us have?

****

No. 424 THE LITERARY DIET

You may well have heard of this term but few pause to think about what it means. Some authors present themselves to the world in bloated multi-volume Collected Works, filling half a shelf or more with their uncontrolled outpourings. This is the classic approach but it leads to weighty tomes and any incautious consumers may end up not only with a hernia but with literary indigestion. What can be done? Here are some tips for healthy and stress-free Writing, without too many Superlatives.

Try to cut out long words. You do not need them. Keep the text short and your style brief. You can still make the same point and tell the same tale. Use 'Tale' rather than 'Narrative'. "Hi!' rather than "Manifold Greetings, I wish you a good morning". 'Plot' has only four letters.

Reduce the number of unnecessary Adjectives, especially the saturated adverbial phrases.

Try to Avoid Verbs. No verbs. No words for actions. No terms for movement. For being. For possession. For behaviour. It can be done.

Dispense with unnecessary Characters. Violently if necessary.

Avoid lengthy and ponderous paragraphs. Gerundives are not necessary and all forms of padding out a text merely lead to overconsumption of space. This is very unhealthy from a creative viewpoint. Repetition leads to flab. Some themes are in themselves 'heavy' and may be best avoided. Religion, Politics, Economic Theory, and so forth. Punctuation need not be excessive – better a semi-colon than a full stop. There are many possible literary excercises.

Expositions, extensions, excursions, expansions, expostulations, experimentations, extrapolations, exculpations, exclamations, excommunications and all other excessive extras – Remember: 'ex' means 'out'. Keep them that way. The 'ex' Factor leads only to distress.

One needs a good Editor; After all, 'Edit' is an anagram of 'Diet'.

Not everyone can manage Power-Writing but a regular rhythm of ten minutes' writing every morning will serve to keep the creative powers flowing and reduce unnecessary verbosity, which is worse than obesity. To reach a Happy Ending one needs directness.

Follow these suggestions and you may yet attain a slim volume.

MORAL:- With some effort, dedication and discipline, Light Reading IS attainable for all!

****

No. 425 CREDITS

Credit is what you give when you believe someone – from the word 'credo' in Latin – "I believe". If a client brings a credible story as to why he buys on credit, it is incredible what some banks will do. One can discredit someone or miscredit them – Debit is Debatable but Misdebit rarely occurs. Banks and countries deal in Credits in Millions and Billions, being apparently always willing to believe. Someone should say one should never give credit where credit is due, but only where it has in the past already been paid off. But how to check the balances? Bankers keep books – sometimes several at a time – but don't read them. Their tastes do not run to literature and what most interests them in a novel are the numbers at the bottom of each page.

One day a man, a writer, went to a Banker and asked to borrow some money so he could live until a publisher paid him for his latest book. The Banker was Interested, because Bankers are always interested in Interest, the rate of their interest usually going up with the rate of Interest. They have a sense for the per-cents. Banks can make something out of nothing – they can make a debt of 100 Pounds into a debt of 150 Pounds within weeks just by adding miscellaneous service charges and compounding their actions with interest – and they can also make Something into Nothing by calling in a loan alone, without consultation. But the last thing a Banker wants to hear is the old saying "Neither a Borrower not a Lender be...." - because they need both. Bankers can change Money but they cannot change themselves.

So this Banker asked the man when he would be prepared to pay the money back. (Some people still think that bank Automatic Cash Machines automatically make Cash, but this is not the case.) The wind of progress can soon turn into an overdraught. The man said he would pay back at the end of the month. The Banker lent him the money and then after three weeks asked for it back, in fact asked for 120 Pounds back immediately. The man said they would have to wait another week until the end of the month, when the Publisher had paid him the advance they had promised in a promissory note. The Bank refused, saying that it was THEIR Money and THEY could decide what to do it and they reduced his Credit Rating from AAAAAAPlus or something pointless like that to D-Minus. The Man was declared Bankrupt, just before the payments for the deal he had made with the Publisher came in and so the Bank could profit royally from the lot, including royalties. For a Profit is of most value when in your own country and especially in your own account on account of the counting. And the only thing that matters is this:

_____ - i.e. the Bottom Line.

The End.

And now it is time for the rolling Credits:

Plot: Walter Rothschild
Plot Developer: Walter Rothschild
Editor: Walter Rothschild
Adviser: Walter Rothschild
2nd. Adviser: Walter Rothschild
Proof Reader: Walter Rothschild
3rd. Assistant Adviser: Walter Rothschild
Climaxes: provided by: Walter Rothschild
Author: Walter Rothschild
Supply of Adjectives: Walter Rothschild

Romance Adviser: Walter Rothschild

Catering: Walter Rothschild
Coffees provided by courtesy of: Walter Rothschild
Spell Checker: Walter Rothschild
Thesaurus: Walter Rothschild
Dictionary Services: Walter Rothschild
Ending by: Walter Rothschild
Location Services: Walter Rothschild.
Printer: Canon
Ink cartridges and Toner provided by Saturn.
Recycled words, Printed on Recycled Paper.

No Intellects or Fantasies were damaged by the reading of this Story.

Based on an original idea by: Walter Rothschild

Any connection or similarity between this Story and any other Story or any Character, fictional or non-fictional, alive or dead, must be a product of your own imagination.

Passed for Reading by: Persons 12 years and upwards.

MORAL:- Well I ask you - Who would credit it?

****

No. 426 A GUIDE TO GROWING BONSAI TREES

A Bonsai tree is a thing of beauty and a joy for the eyes, although admittedly you do need very good eyesight. They have been selectively bred over centuries to keep their height as low as possible and to get the branches to spread out. Many people enjoy keeping some of these wonderful specimens on their balconies or window ledges.

You will need a plant pot of suitable small size and some soil and fertilizer and a place with enough light, south facing if possible. The soil should be light with maybe half a handful of fine sand adding to a mulch formed of well-matured vegetable compost (preferably peas and lentils) and a few fine wood shavings, or sawdust, preferably from pine or cedar due to the acidity. Important is to keep all quantities very small, otherwise the root system can become over-burdened with the overburden. For example, the term 'handful' refers to a small hand, such as that of a young child.

The shoot must be watered regularly – once per day - but with only a few drops at a time.

A new mode is the 'Bionsai' range for biologically grown plants using as manure the dung from especially-bred Dung Beetles. This also attracts fruit flies which are about the right size for the trees. The leaves, when they fall in the autumn, can be gathered and used as "bio tree tea leaves". However this is to be drunk only in small cups, such as those used in dolls' houses.

Should, despite all efforts, the trees die, their trunks can be re-used as lollipop sticks.

MORAL:- Size isn't Everything. But sometimes you do need a good magnifying glass.

****

No. 427 HAPPY HOUR

Some stories are best read at Literary Cafés. The trouble is that Cafés have their own rules and ambience and this is often but not always helpful.

From 5pm to 6pm is 'Happy Hour' and you can read twice as many words for the same price.

SOMETIMES THE NOISE OF THE MUSIC

The only problem is that the place fills up with people wanting cheap words and chatter, and while

IS VERY LOUD AND YOU CANNOT

you are in the middle A tries to talk to B with limited success, you can barely make out a word they are saying

MAKE YOURSELF HEARD AT ALL

and it is a time of day when a lot of shrill office workers escape their boring daytime

BECAUSE THE LOUDSPEAKERS ARE

jobs and like to spread themselves around and chat noisily and flirt with each other and

SENDING PULSATING WAVES OF

gossip nastily about their bosses and even more nastily about their colleagues (especially that

SOUND RIGHT ACROSS THE STREET,

BITCH of a Supervisor, do you know what she said to me?) - which is why this is called

EXCUSE ME WHILE I TURN IT OFF.

the Happy Hour, the hour when one can get happily tipsy and happily relaxed and be

OH; THAT IS SO MUCH BETTER.....

happy about the fact that work is over for the day. And when the Work is over one can open a nice book and envelop yourself in the story, sink gently into the narrative, enjoy the twists of the plots, consider idly how the story might develop and whether all the characters will make it to the end. Of course the people around you will still be chattering inanely about their trivial pursuits and their pursuit of the trivial and at some point a waiter or writer (there is only one letter difference and many of them are in any case the latter trying to earn a crust as the former) will come by, wipe the desk demonstratively, shuffle the paperbacks and ask if there is another chapter or something you might like? – a polite way of indicating that during 'Happy Hour' space is at a premium and other people are waiting for your book, whether or not you have reached The End. So enjoy it while you can, get as far forward in the Story as you can, and what I would really recommend is to come back when it is quieter, when everyone else will be (by definition) Unhappy but You at least will be able at last to stretch out and turn over the pages at leisure with less risk of being disturbed by anything but the more violent scenes with the blood and the gore around Chapter 14. And a Happy End is always SO much better than a mere Happy Hour.

MORAL:- With a good book, a Happy Hour can last an eternity.....

****

No. 428 THE RECIPE

To Prepare a **Short Story:**

EITHER: Take one piece of Paper, one Pen, filled with black or blue-black Ink.

OR: One standard-sized Keyboard and Screen, plus a Printer with Black Ink Cartridge.

Take one Idea, three Sub-Ideas, one Plot, three Sub-Plots. Turn Idea over in one's mind for a period of time. If Historical Research is necessary, use the keyboard. Facts can be Wikified into a Goo-Gel.

Compose Three Paragraphs of medium size; Introduce the main Characters singly, providing descriptions; Then Stir the Characters together and ensure plenty of time for inter-reaction. Allow the Plot to develop and the tension to rise for at least 8 pages.

Add Conflict and Love Interest (2 Portions for added depth, but remove all Flesh references unless preparing Adult Literature. Usually Three Pages of Spiced Romance suffice for stories intended for those interested more in Romantics than Antics.)

For extra Colour add some new locations and descriptive passages, with Comparative and Superlative adjectival supplements. (Not too many). Scatter Hints over the surface.

Allow Plot to thicken further and simmer over up to ten pages. Check regularly for Spelling Mistakes. Prepare Layout and separated indented Paragraphs.

Avoid any half-baked Ideas, or tasteless Additives. Beware of corrupt Accountants who may overcook the Books.

Deliver to Publisher and Cross Fingers.

MORAL:- Much is a matter of Taste. But it is better not to rush.

****

No. 429 GOLDILOCKS AND THE THREE BEARS: THE FILM

"All right – Take 1. Start."

"Once upon a time there were three bears, er.."

"CUT!

Start again! Take 2."

"Once upon a time there were three bears, Daddy Bear, Mummy Bear and -"

"CUT – too old fashioned. How about two Daddy Bears? Must it be three bears?"

"Yes. This is what it says here in the text. The traditional text."

"Oh well, if you say so. But I'm not sure what our sponsor will make of this. All ready? Take 3. Start."

"Once upon a time there were three bears, Daddy Bear, Mummy Be-"

"CUT! Yes, what is it?"

"Boss, Head Office says Jane Hinslett cannot make it so we've signed Suzy Dish instead – but she is a brunette. Can we make it Brownilocks and the Several Bears?"

"Oh shoot. That'll mean altering the publicity as well. And the background lyrics. AND the merchandising. Don't like it. Can she dye her hair for this story?"

"Good idea, Boss. I'll call back and suggest that."

"Good, now, back to the action. All ready? Pages turned? Take 4:"

"Once upon a time there were three bears; Daddy Bear, Mummy Bear and Baby Bear. They lived in a house in the woods."

"CUT, Good, I like it. Super. Now we need an exterior shot, OK? House in the woods. Props?"

"Ready, Boss."

"OK, so, let's see, the Bears, they go into the house, right? In order, right? Daddy, Mummy and Baby? Yes, ready? Scene Two, Take 1. Go."

"One day Daddy Bear, Mummy Bear and Baby Bear went into their house in the woods."

"CUT. Too slow. They need to walk in quicker, right? They're hungry, they know their porridge is waiting? Getting cold? I want to see some movement here, some hurrying, get me? Take 2."

"OnedayDaddyBearMummyBearandBabyBearwentintotheirhousein thewoods."

"CUT. That's better. Now repeat but this time, when they go through the door, they go straight to the table, OK? Take 3."

"OnedayDaddyBearMummyBearandBabyBearwentintotheirhousein thewoods, and went to sit at the table."

"Print. OK, now we need the same shot from the back. Backwards, OK?"

"Er..."

"Come ON, this is easy. Just read it backwards, we see them from the rear, right? Take 3."

"sdoow eht ni esuoh rieht otni tnew reaB ybaB dna reaB ymmuM reaB yddaD yad enO."

"Got that? Tone, Volume? Good, that's good. I like it. Good. Now, let's skip to Chapter 3."

"But..."

"Well, we probably won't need this opening sequence in any case. We're just taking it now in case, right. All right everybody, Chapter three, Goldilocks, hair all right? OK, blonde wig, right? Now, let the strap of your dress down a bit further, more, more, that's right, just so. And when you wake up, smile nicely at Daddy Bear, OK? Yeah, you get me. All right, everyone, take your places....."

MORAL:- All that glitters is not necessary a Golden Oscar.

****

71

No. 430 THE PACKAGING

*****STORYOPOLIN NARRATIVA 1Pg.*****

INSTRUCTIONS.

Before Reading this Story, Read the Story fully to the End.

This Story contains: Narrative, Plot, Characters, Traces of Humour, Elements of Punctuation.

There are No Illustrations.

This Story may be absorbed optically or (with assistance from another Reader) aurally; It is not suitable for Injection. Braille versions are not yet in production.

DOSAGE.

The Story is provided in Pages. Open each numbered Page separately.

Take one Word at a time, forming into Sentences and Paragraphs. If necessary, repeat several times until one can understand the Plot.

It is permitted to break the Story into several sections and take pauses for a Cup of Tea.

For Children: An Adult should read the Story Aloud at Bedtime until Sleep occurs naturally.

COUNTER INDICATIONS.

DO NOT Read this Story if you are-

Suffering from Analphabetism or Dyslexia

Unable to read English

Have an Allergy to Humour

Suffer from Tired Eyes

Wishing to become Pregnant*

Easily Bored

Stylistically Hypercritical

Driving a Motor Vehicle (especially HGV)

POSSIBLE SIDE EFFECTS

Research indicates the following potential Side Effects of Reading this Story:

Mild Confusion   (1 in 10,000)

Mild attacks of Laughter (1 in 100,000)

Impatience
Narcoleptic Reactions, Heavy Eyelids, Loss of Interest

If in doubt, consult a Literary Critic immediately.

STORAGE.
Keep the Story in a flat place away from the light, preferably within a Book on a Shelf. Take out and open only when necessary for Reading.
This PIL (Patient Information Leaflet) is to be kept folded tightly vertically and horizontally twelve times over and placed in the Book as a Bookmark that is too fiddly ever to unfold properly or, once unfolded, too difficult to fold together again and replaced where it came from.

- -

(All Rights © Literary Pharmaceuticals n.V. Ede-Wageningen NL) Note: The Small Print is designed just to fill the bottom part of the instructions sheet with a text that is so small that it serves no real purpose whatsoever but at least makes it look as though expensive lawyers can be used against you should you ever wish to consider complaining about anything at all so it is better not to do so and just accept your utter and total powerlessness as Consumer. In consequence nobody ever actually reads it but it must always be there. The text has been checked for spelling irregularities.

- • If you wish to become pregnant, Stop ALL Reading and just get on with it.

  ****

Feng Shui is the ancient traditional

Chinese art of establishing
patterns   whereby the

furniture or other

objects are

                                      placed   in   specific
places so as

                                      to interact

                              in the exchange of
                                  energy
                                              and   are
oriented
                                              so   as   to
find places
                                              with   good
'*Qi*'

          You   will
not
find
                                      Qi
   in a   dark
cave
       not even
a
                      Qi   hole.

Ask a good consultant to tell
                              you
                where to put
                                        the next words and
                especially
                        the END.

MORAL:- There is a Place for Everything and Everything should have its Place. That is the *Qi* to
                Inner Happiness.

****

No. 432 THE HACKER

We refer to a modern plague, to the pirates of the computer age, those who invade and ravage and destroy. A Hacker is the term used for a person who, for reasons of plain boredom or perhaps just to show off what he can do, or for reasons of pure malevolence decides to break into the private correspondence of other people or of institutions and either steal the data or deliberately block and warp and twist the texts and figures so as to make them unusable. This is of course infuriating for the person whose work is now ruined or stolen or blocked off from use, or whose bank details have been stolen, and in their helplessness and frustration they can swear and rage and have seizures whilst on the screen in front of them they see something like this:

7	9	5	3	8	6	2	8	7
8	5							
6	3	1	9	5	2	8	7	5
3	9							
2	6	4	3	0	7	6	5	5
3	3							
8	7	4	9	3	1	8	6	3
8	5							
9	1	6	3	2	8	5	7	6
3	5							
2	8	5	4	1	9	6	8	4
8	8							

but moving downwards all the time and sometimes silly pictures or faces or voices taunting them from the distant ethereal and unreal wastelands of the Black Cloud. In such cases the virtues of virtual reality are overwhelmed by the STOPSTOP hey, I didn't write this, what's happening? HAH HAH HAH! Oh no, I fear something is happening to this computer YESYESYOUFOOLHAH HAH!! Quick! I must swit-
XXXXXXXXXXXXXXXXXXXXXXXXXXXXXXXXXXXXXXXXXX
3th 34t2üo3it rf qsdcsjdqöwfq n3rit qwdav+wo b+gf1 +2ir kjkjkz12t,,,;;;ähtz34 rfjajfa ha fawdf awrf oirt qir twiw58 zw845zwgkejfa kwedj JSDKJVAFO$QN§$T NQFJAWED
        jowief f wf wrf wurpwerhgwieuw tdf ghbub hu er eq weTTFGHTweief   wf   wpof   wpof   gb   casPSD
        OQDCQÜPBRHZGFCRRWOEppüppasjoiwdhehrügw
egwe

MORAL:- You don't really need Balls to be a hacker – so if you catch one, you'll know what you can do to him......

No. 433 COLOUR BLINDNESS

The human eye is a wondrous organ; through the pupil and the iris and the innumerable nerve endings that link this light-sensitive organ to the brain, and actually in duplicate to allow for bifocal orientation, balance and the calculation of speed and distance, the eye brings to its owner what is quaintly called the 'gift' of sight. An oculist or an ocular surgeon (one who does not need binoculars to see what he is doing) could no doubt describe much more accurately than I exactly what it is inside that squishy jelly-like substance that fills those holes in our skulls and yet never falls out (which would be rather embarrassing and probably an eye-sore). There is fluid in the eyes and pressure, but the cataracts are very different to normal waterfalls.

(Incidentally the River Nile has four sets of Catarcts as it flows from the Sudan from Khartoum northwards. Hence the term Nile-ism. But there are no Qatar-Acts as Qatar does not have large rivers.)

There are eyes which are dark and eyes which are light, eyes which have brown pupils and blue and grey-ish and even green ones. (There are Schools which have coloured pupils too, but unfortunately often this is a cause for local controversy, additional teaching staff and even Special Measures.) There are eyes which are somehow squashed horizontally for Oriental persons – they do not open vertically as far as do those of Occidental persons, which is surely no occident. Felines and snakes have very different mechanisms for protecting the surface of the eye through the eye lids. There is indeed a lot one can say about the Eyes. Some people sleep with pads over their eyes to keep out the light – eye-pads – whereas others just close their eyes and find themselves drifting off to sleep where, with their Inner Eye, they can still see what they are dreaming about – the brain "sees" things even if the eyelids are closed. Most strange. It seems as though the brain has a long list of things to work through at a time when it is not bothered by external imagery, and so these subjects are stacked up in a sequence somewhere in the brain and await their turn to be examined – forming an Eye Queue.

In human society a very important acquired skill is 'selective blindness', a means of simply not seeing what one does not wish to see – whether this be poverty or oppression or injustice or a person in the room with whom one does not wish to exchange greetings.... Anglers, who develop a sort of fish-eye lens when they stand for long hours in waders or squatting on uncomfortable folding stools on river banks, will often "cast an eye" on their float to see where a potential catch may be lurking in the water – to "catch an eye". There are those who, being unable to read the letters of the alphabet, never understand the point of an i – or better said, the point ON the i. For the Saxons an Eye was a piece of ground surrounded by swamp or fen – what we now call an Eye-Land.

But one element which is especially curious is how each of us sees the phenomenon of Colour. Now, Colour can be caused by various means – refractions in beams of light for example, the heaviness of the atmosphere that lets the evening light turn golden rather than bright white; There are complex issues of differing wavelengths and the way they are received by 'receptor cones' retained in the retinas. It is possible that when I say a specific shade is 'Red' that no two of us actually see or experience the same thing – (hence the phrase "eye two eye") but there is simply no way to compare! All we can say with some degree of certainty is that "The Eyes have it!"

But there are people whose eyes are unable to distinguish certain colours. Where what we laughingly call 'normal' people see red and yellow, orange and violet, blue and green, a whole spectrum of colours – like these, for example – they see only black and white. It is very sad – they are unable to appreciate the glories of a sunset or a sunrise, of a bed of flowers, of the different shades of their partner's hair, of the clothes that we are wearing – just look for example at these wonderful colourful letters in which this text is being printed right now. No, they see only black letters against a white background, thus missing out on so many of the wonders of the Universe.

I do hope that you, dear readers, will have some sympathy for these people and not mock them. Sometimes, it seems, such Colour Blindness – the technical term for this affliction – is only temporary, it comes and goes; One can look at the blue sky, the green grass, a glass of red wine, and then pick up a piece of paper like this one and yet – suddenly – the ability to see the colours has gone! Even if this hits one only for a brief while, this is a distressing occurrence. Clearly more research is necessary – I believe the major industrial concern Eye-See-Eye is working on some chemical solutions right now.

So, for now, relax, sit back, look carefully at this text and enjoy the colours!

MORAL:- There many insights in sights. If necessary, one may need to exchange an Eye for an Eye.

****

No. 434 THE RETURN TICKET

A man went to the Ticket Office and asked for a Return Ticket. "Yes sir, Where to?" asked the Ticket Clerk politely. The man was nonplussed. (Note, this is NOT the same as being Minussed.)

"Well, actually I want to return back to Here," he explained.

The Ticket Clerk sighed and said, "In that case, Sir, I can offer you a Ticket in two Halves – one Half for Getting to your Destination, and the other for Returning. Would that be in order?"

"Why, thank you" said the man and was satisfied. It didn't seem to matter where the ticket was made out to, what was important to him was the feeling that he could still come Home again afterwards; This assured him stability and a sense of permanence and calm. If you think about it, this is a very sensible view of life. There are hundreds and thousands of places one could theoretically go to, if one wanted to, or if one had to – for work or for a meeting or to get something or to run away from something or from someone – but actually the one place we All want to go to, deep down inside ourselves, is Back Here.

For some people their destination is their destiny. There are Destinationalists who believe that their nation is their destiny and even Transdestinationalists who feel that their nation is Everyone's destiny whether they want it to be so or not. Some people like stillness, and still waters which run deep, whilst others prefer destilled liquids which can run even deeper before rising to the head in a destabilising way.

So he handed over his credit card and the Ticket Clerk performed some electronic magic with it by swiping it through a slot and the machine went "clatter clatter clatter" and a piece of criss-crossed coloured paper came out and on it was this text.

The Ticket read as follows.

OUTWARD
PAID

Date: *TODAY.*   From: ....*HERE*....... To ....*THERE*......

                              [Via: ......*ON THE* *WAY*......................]

           Valid: **ALL DAY.**

                              ONE PERSON.

- -

RETURN
DIAP

WORROMOT :etaD   *EREH KCAB*...........:oT
.....*EREHT*..... :morF

                              [.....*YAW* *EHT*
NO....................]

           YAD LLA : dilaV

                              NOSREP EMAS EHT

And with this Ticket in his pocket the man went cheerfully out from the Ticket Office, ready to go anywhere in the Big Wide World that might appeal to him, anywhere indeed that he could reach in a day, knowing securely deep in his heart that he could come back Home afterwards.

Which is, actually one of the best definitions of Happiness one can think of!

****

Walter Rothschild ./. dlihcshtoR retlaW
18.12.2016 (ALL DAY ROVER)

No. 435.   THE DELIVERY.

INTL. NARRATIVE DELIVERY SERVICES INC.

Dear Reader!

We are sorry to inform you that we could not deliver the Story you considered Reading. This could have been because

- You were out

- You were out of your mind

- You were not concentrating

- You could not find the Book or the Page

- You dropped the Book and lost your place

The Story will be made available at your local Library at:

.......□□□□□□ □□□□□□ □□□·...........

On Tuesdays between 15.30 and 16.15. In the Fiction Department, Shelves C-D.

We apologise for any inconvenience caused. Should you have any complaint, e.g. That you were awake and concentrating all the time, please contact our Readers' Service Hotline on:

00+91-471-86652076157

[Please note: This Call Service Centre is situated for your convenience in Thiruvananthapuram, Kerala, India and so you need to call between 01.00 and 03.00 European Time.]

Stories may be found in Books, Magazines, Albums, Online.

We thank you for ordering your Story from us and trust you will enjoy your Reading and will recommend us to your friends if you have any.

No. 436 HYPNOSIS

Hypnosis is an art, or a science – some would say a pseudo-science – whereby a person is influenced by external stimuli, say a voice repeating certain phrases, or through observing repetitive movements, into entering a trance-like state where he or she can be subjected to 'suggestions' placed directly into their subconscious and so behave in a trance in a manner at odds with their normal clear, wakeful, semi-rational self. (One says 'semi-rational' because we speak here of *Homo Sapiens*; only Dolphins are wholly rational mammals.) The term comes from the Greek word *"hupnos"* for 'sleep', probably because many schoolboys found that Greek lessons at school put them gently to sleep. (There is the phrase 'Latin Lovers' but no-one ever speaks of a 'Greek Lover').

As in all such 'arts' there is a technique, a technique which needs to be mastered if success is to be attained. Some practitioners employ this technique for therapeutic purposes, to enable a patient to be calmed down and to regress into childhood or even beyond – some would claim, even into pre-birth experiences and others will even claim, into previous lives. Can one believe this? It is an excellent question – can one believe ANYTHING these days or even those days? The fact is that a sleeping person inhabits a different universe both temporal and spatial than does a wakeful person, and those who are daydreaming, on the cusp between wakefulness and sleep, are a bit in this one and a bit in that one, with flashbacks and flash-forwards and sudden changes of theme and subject and pace. Sleep is not always peaceful, but it is always sleep. But under Hypnosis one is NOT asleep, one can function as a normal wakeful person, speaking, answering questions, performing normal movements – and sometimes moving beyond such normal speech and actions. Some practitioners perform Hypnosis on the stage, asking volunteers from the audience to step forward and be placed under the 'hypnotic influence' – they are literally 'entranced' – and while in a trance they will then perform all sorts of bizarre actions on command and, on being woken from the trance, will have no conscious memory of it whatsoever. Clearly a part of the brain is being reached and activated – and other controlling or critical parts de-activated – and even memory being wiped out on command by the person controlling the procedure – the Hypnotist.

Let us now try a little experiment:

You are now reading this sentence slowly from left to right across the page

You are now reading this sentence slowly from left to right across the page

You are now reading this sentence slowly from left to right across the page

You are now reading this sentence slowly from left to right across the page

You are now reading this sentence slowly from left to right across the page

You are now reading this sentence slowly from left to right across the page

You are now reading this sentence slowly from left to right across the page

You are now reading this sentence slowly from left to right across the page

You are now reading this sentence slowly from left to right
across the page

You are now reading this sentence slowly from left to right
across the page

You are now reading this sentence slowly from left to right
across the page

You are now reading this sentence slowly from left to right
across the page

You are now reading this sentence slowly from left to right
across the page

You are now reading this sentence slowly from left to right
across the page

You are now reading this sentence slowly from left to right
across the page

It is a wonderful story and you will download and buy it
when you wake up

It is a wonderful story and you will download and buy it
when you wake up

It is a wonderful story and you will download and buy it
when you wake up

It is a wonderful story and you will download and buy it
when you wake up

It is a wonderful story and you will download and buy it
when you wake up

It is a wonderful story and you will download and buy it
when you wake up

It is a wonderful story and you will download and buy it
when you wake up

It is a wonderful story and you will download and buy it
when you wake up

It is a wonderful story and you will download and buy it
when you wake up

Now when you read this sentence to the end and come to the words 'Wake Up' you will wake up. **WAKE UP!!** Good! You have enjoyed a fascinating read, you have learned a lot and you will recommend this Story to all your friends.

MORAL:- This is one way to improve sales figures.

****

No. 437 THE FIRST READING LESSON

First, let's make sure you are sitting comfortably. Are you sitting comfortably? Can you see all right? Are you upright enough? Very well. Let us start.

Open the Book to the first Page. With your eyes, Engage the First Paragraph. Look around – forwards and backwards. Are there any texts you have overlooked, apart from Contents and Publisher? Title Page? Are you ready? Then let us read on. In your own time, let your eyes engage and move forward across the lines. Left to right, then pause, check, then the next line, left to right. Are you ready? Then the third line. It gets easier with practice, once you get the hang of it.

Not too fast, not too fast, go easy. We are NOT in a rush. Understand? We are NEVER in a rush. We do NOT rush. This would be foolish and might lead to your skipping a line by mistake and not understanding what is going on. Reading under the Influence of Incomprehension. Next thing you know, you'll be Skip-Reading, just flipping through the pages. Don't do that, it makes you blind, you know. And then you'll be left only with Audio Books. Not like the real thing at all.

Very well. That got us into the Second Paragraph and through it as well. Now, in your own time, engage with the Third Paragraph. The story should be flowing smoothly by now, yes? Left to right, pause, down, left to right, pause, down, left to right, that's right, you are doing well. Keep looking ahead, you must never lose sight of the bottom of the Page. Can you see the Number at the bottom yet? Well, that means you are getting closer. Take your time, we want you to enjoy the experience, read carefully, absorb the Story. One Page at a time.

Good, now, we are coming up soon to a Chapter Break. Do you remember what to do? Slow down, pause, reflect a little on what you have read, can you recall it clearly? If necessary, look back again, before starting the next Chapter. Now, Look at the Heading first. That will show you which direction to go. Ready? Very well, Chapter Two. Now, start slowly again, yes, look around, in your own time, ready, now. I can see you are getting the hang of this, but don't, DON'T get over-confident. There are still several complex punctuation points and unusual grammatical forms you will have to learn before you can tackle a thicker book. Not to mention Footnotes and Endnotes. But you are doing well. Just pace yourself. It is not about speed. That's right, left to right, pause, down, and left to right again, and pause and look, we are coming up to some Brackets, (take care with these, they always come in Pairs, have we got to the closing one yet? Ah yes) – good, now do you see this Question Mark? That means you have to raise the tone (or pitch, as we call it) a little when reading aloud, into an interrogative. When you read to yourself it's the same, but silent.

A tricky bit coming up here. You have reached the last line. Left to right, then pause, no, do not read the number, but keep in your mind what the last words were. Now, With your right thumb and forefinger take hold gently of the upper right-hand corner of the Page. Upper right. Yes, gently, gently, do you feel you have it held firmly? Then swing the right arm across to the left and let go – not too soon! Not too soon! Then it will fall back. A bit more, yes, that's right. Good.

You have turned your first Page! That's always a bit of a milestone, I find. Now you can see, the text continues. Proceed. Just as before. Don't worry that you are now reading on the Left whereas on the previous Page you were on the Right. Most modern books have this Bipagination, both sides of the Page are printed on. You may need to adjust your seat slightly, or turn your body a little to the left. Is that all right?

Good. Now then, maybe it is time to move on a little faster. But just a little. Sometimes there are unexpected Twists to a Plot and then you need to exercise due care and attention. But for now things seem calm. So keep going. Left to right, pause, down, and continue till the end of – Oh Look Out!! There's a Surprise Ending coming up! Quick! No, too la.......

MORAL:- Never assume a Happy Ending. And no-one has ever decrypted the Highway Code.

****

No. 438 STATISTICS

Statistics have been collected for rulers, kings and government administrations for 4,372 years. (According to some sources, 4,374). At present 31,874 persons are occupied full-time with collecting statistics for the Government. They work in 2,997 offices in 375 buildings and an additional 267 sub-branches. They have worked a total of 1,880,639.45 hours each month collecting and collating and analysing statistics.

These statistics are then passed on to the civil servants responsible for arranging for meetings to be held at departmental level to discuss possible moves to take initiatives on a conditional basis – subject to budget - if and when the time appears to be right on the basis of the information available and if this is considered absolutely necessary for political reasons, in which case inter-departmental meetings would need to be arranged as the diary permits to allow the entire process to be repeated, dependent on funding which itself will be affected by interest rates, rate of inflation calculated back to the beginning of the previous year and the current Stock Exchange Index, plus a percentage for reserves and unforeseen eventualities. At this stage an average (January – June) of 73.2% of the statistics are discarded and the remainder have to be padded to fill the resultant gaps. They are then published in Statistical Reports, to which the Opposition in Parliament makes sarcastical Statistical Retorts.

The 17 Ministers and 28 Deputy Ministers in charge of their respective Ministries have studied these statistics for a joint cumulative total of 162 seconds and they have been discussed at Cabinet for a total of 6 minutes and 13 seconds. Most of the Ministers are technically innumerate, which is why they cannot cope with the concept of proportional voting and require electoral agents to arrange purchase of the necessary votes in their consistent constituencies. Indeed it has been said that since the average politician has only one arse but two elbows, they are congenitally handicapped from resolving statistical inconsistencies. There have of course been several recent scandals when a politician has been exposed for allegedly massaging or being massaged by Statistics, usually of the vital 36 – 24 – 36 variety.

Statistics fall into the categories Convenient (12.8%), Inconvenient (54.32%), Dangerous/Embarrassing (46.7%), Accurate (0.03%) and Fictitious (72.1%). Statistics are rarely static and even less likely to make one ecstatic. Statisticians do not actually DO anything, they just count the number of people who are doing something or the number of somethings they have done. This they class as 'Work'. They are more interested in fractions than factions, though they often end up with fictions that cause frictions if not fractiousness. In many cases however (up to 82.3% of cases) Statistics are welcomed by their recipients since they usually say what the recipients want to read and so reinforce current policies. For statisticians, the decimal point is the only point they can see and understand and per cents form the only sense they sense at all.

MORAL:- It has been statistically proven that some 118.35% of official government statistics are inaccurate, to such an extent that it would be a lie to call them mere lies or even damned lies.

****

No. 439 THE APO'STRO'PHE

There was once an Apostrophe who was sick of being misused. "No'one cares any more," he said. "They think they can just stick any bit of punctuation wherever they want, and no-one will take any no'tice. The situation is apostrophous. I went to a Grammar School and I learned the proper procedures.

I have a place and I know my place. Why doesn't anyone else? It's, like, where a vowel elides, right? 'Do Not' becomes 'Don't', not 'Donut'. 'Will not' becomes 'won't'. 'Shall not' becomes 'Shan't' – a tricky one as the ells elllllllide too. Then there are the possessives – mine and yours don't need me of course, nor do his and hers or theirs, but if it's John's or Jane's..... then you need me!

Either they miss me out completely or they stick me where I don't belong," he complained. Apostrophes like complaining but, let's be honest, they've good reason for doing so. There is an apocryphal story of one who got itself embedded repeatedly between a rock and a hard place, ending up with "rock'n'ardplace".

"I hate it also when people are too lazy with Plurals. How often do you see 'Dolly's" for 'Dollies, and even "Holiday's" for "Holidays"? They just stick one of me in without thinking through what they are (or they're) trying to say. I've seen "2 Pound's of Carrot's" – truly! It's unbelievable. 'If in doubt, just use an extra ap'ostrophe' – that's all they'll think of. Then you've got theologians with their Apostrophical Succession – a whole succession of Apostrophes where they're not really needed for liturgical purposes – debating *homo'ousia* and *homoi'ousia* - and then some modern idiots think the Apps on their Smartphones are also short for Apostrophes. You get sportsmen who mix me up with Trophies. (Or trophy's – sportsmen are notorious for accelerated illiteracy). Grammar has been commacialised these days, colons are full of excrement and semi-colons are hardly better. It's dis'gus'ting!"

A passing Hyphen stopped to remonstrate with him but began to hyper-hyphenate and said "I must dash, before I go Infinite", adding an Exclamation Mark for good measure. "Do you post rough, or would you rather fancy a rough Postie?" was his parting shot.

The Apostrophe stormed off stroppily. "He lied," he thought. He had his pride, and would rather get laid than elide.

<u>MO'RAL</u>:-   Don't worry, there's not much poin't in punctuation.

****

No. 440   3D

Over the years we have seen many attempts to make cooking easier and quicker. If you think about it, once upon a time in the distant past our ancestors had to chase over the Veld to spear a mammoth or any other mammal that could not run faster than they could or was not more intelligent than they and so less able to avoid a trap. Evolution saw to it that the less intelligent animals were eaten and the less intelligent humans got nothing to eat and so left the gene pool.

But then they had to cut into the animal's hide and slice off chunks of bloody flesh and eventually learned to hang these chunks on a spit over a wooden camp fire so as to roast the raw flesh. And so the steak and the chop and even the spare rib was born.

Later developments saw the growth of vegetables in the diet. Other ancestors had to set out across dangerous waters in primitive and makeshift vessels to catch and later eat fish before they were themselves caught and eaten by the fish..... Someone once had the brilliant idea of smashing bits of grass between stones and taking the resultant powder, mixing it with water, letting some invisible yeast spores from the air arrive, put it into an enclosed clay chamber with a fire underneath, and - voilà! - there was Bread. Man does not live by Bread alone, as has been already stated, but nevertheless to live without it is also difficult and unsatisfying. Scholars may argue whether it was the ancient Rabbi Hillel or the Earl of Sandwich who first thought of placing a filling between two slices of the new wonder material but, either way, this has remained a staple of most western civilisations ever since – these being civilisations based upon wheat and grains rather than rice and beans. Some academic institutions even offer Sandwich Courses to provide qualifications in the preparation of such comestibles.

The domestication of some mammals (mammals being creatures which provide milk as well as meat) led to various uses being found for milk from especially cows and goats (but also sheep and yaks). Milk could be drunk, spun and stirred until it turned into butter, or treated with enzymes from the air to become yoghurt or allowed to harden, stiffened with rennet made from bits of animal intestine and – thanks to different spores – turn into dangerous-looking solid (or runny) cheeses.

These inventions were all made so long ago that no-one thinks of them any more and just assumes that these foods were always there – but no, they were not always there, someone had the idea and pursued it, maybe experimented a bit, maybe had some failures – burnt meat and burnt toast, poisonous cheeses.....

The invention of Restaurants allowed people to come into a private room and let someone else cook for them – against payment. Almost a form of culinary brothel, the cook would do almost whatever one asked – for a fixed price.

Then came Takeaway or Take-Away food – one had simply to walk down to some establishment on the corner of the street and purchase a large, hot and nourishing portion of fish and chips and take it home with you or eat it out of some sheets of newspaper in the street, on a bench, wherever. As Mathematics became better understood Pie was also offered and even for the vowelly-challenged Pie-and-Peas.

Nowadays there is a sudden flourish of new Customer Service ideas. Rather than 'Take-Away' there is 'Bring to You'..... Initially one could telephone a local Pizzeria or similar and within a period of time – say, a quarter of an hour – a courier could bring the order to your door. This meant a lot of work for young underpaid couriers on bicycles or mopeds or small delivery vans. The next development owed its origin to the arrival of the internet - One goes online and orders a meal in writing, by e-mail rather than by telephone call. Then some supermarket chains found ways to expand turnover by offering to send an underpaid student round the aisles and collect in a basket the tins and packets that were desired and ordered by individual customers........ and bring it to their homes; This saving these housebound, busy or simply lazy and obese persons the necessity of carrying a shopping bag for themselves. The next stage was to aim up-market and offer the customers fresh produce, especially fresh vegetable and salads, which would enable one to cook a tasty meal for oneself (and if possible one's partner or at least the person one hoped would become a partner, if only for the night) – without all the bother of having to go out shopping to the market oneself.

The newest idea is 'Tweet'n'Eat'. Why go to all the bother of going out to a shop? Or telephoning an order to a shop? Or e-mailing an order to a courier service that will bring you your weekly shoppping from the supermarket or the greengrocer's? Why wait impatiently and hungrily for up to ten whole minutes for a chap to come and ring your bell and deliver a big cardboard box?

New technology now allows food to be ordered online and DELIVERED online – this is the breakthrough. Thanks to the development of 3D Printers one can, for example, order a pizza, pay by PayPal or through your mobile phone account and then print out a pizza on your own desk.

There are still some teething problems to be dealt with. For example, the first is that the range of colours has to be changed from the normal colour range – marketing experts counselled against use of the word 'Cyanide' for Blue. So now one has – as well as Black – Red, Green and Yellow. This means that Blueberries tend to come out rather dark. But otherwise this is not such a big problem.

Then there is the vexed issue of Flavour. Some experimental versions of the 3D printer had a framework attachment for a second supplementary range of cartridges for Beef, Raspberry, Orange, Tuna. The trouble has been that each cartridge would run out after about two items – say, tins of beans or pizzas – and they cost €79.99 each. But then after extensive trials and marketing surveys it was decided that most people who ordered takeaway or home-delivered food, especially pizza or sushi, were not concerned much about Flavour or Taste in any case. A large bottle of Ketchup or Soy Sauce was all that was necessary and if everything else tasted of cardboard, well, the customers were used to this already.

There remain problems with the creation of online Sauces – these tend to use up almost an entire cartridge of liquid each time and this is both expensive and inconvenient, albeit it ensures constant freshness. But once these problems and wrinkles can be resolved there is clearly nothing to stop this next big change in the labour-saving and economising Digestion Market and we are convinced 'Tweet'n'Eat' will become the new rage. Soon there will be no need to get out of bed at all!

<u>MORAL</u>:- Some day my print will come.

****

No. 441 THE INTELLIGENCE TEST

Please take just a few minutes to complete the following Intelligence Test.

1. Which of these sentences is incorrect?
-         There is a God
-         There is a God
-         There is a God.

2. Which is the false entry in the following sequence?
-         1, 2, 3, 4, 5, 6, 7, 8, 9, 10.

3. A is two years older than B, who is three years younger than C, who used to be married to D but left her when he discovered she had lied about her age and was in fact twice that of A minus 5. E will be entitled to take Early Retirement in four years. How old is F?

4. Perform the following calculation in your head: $753 \times 98.3 + 249 - (13^2) \times 17\frac{3}{4} + 1,066$.
 How long did it take you? In Seconds:

6. A man stands in a line of customers at a store. The line moves forward at an average rate of two persons per minute. He calculates that there are 43 people ahead of him. How long will it take him to think "I, Q?" and move elsewhere?

7. A Circle has two sides – the inside and the outside. Calculate the space between them, assuming use of a 2H pencil.

8. What is the square root of a Box Tree?

MORAL:- Let's be honest: If you really had any Intelligence, you wouldn't have wasted so much time on this test.

****

Answers: 1. God Knows. 2. 10 – it has two digits. 3. Who cares? 4. Anything under 400 and you were cheating. 5. Did you notice 5 was missing? 6. It depends what they are queuing for. 7. Ensure you have lead in your pencil. 8. Think outside the Box.

No. 442 APOLOGY

May we have your attention please. This is an Important Announcement for all Readers of this Story currently on Page One. We regret that the commencement of this Story has been delayed by five Paragraphs. This is due to the late arrival of any ideas and authorial shortcomings beyond our control. We shall keep you informed of any further Delays.

This is an Important Announcement for Readers who are impatient to finish the Story and think they already know how it will end; Please report at the Reader Information Desk with your current Page Reference and your book will be re-booked, free of charge.

You will also receive a complimentary Coupon worth 10 Pages towards your next Story.

May we have your attention please. Readers Please turn to the Contents Page and you will see the revised Order of Chapters.

May we have your attention please. This is a Page Change. This is an important Announcement for Readers at the Beginning of Chapter One. Please go instead to Chapter Three and start there instead.

May we have your attention please. This is an Important Announcemenent for all Readers who are expecting a Happy Ending and a Sequel. For details of your ongoing Sequels, Please go straight to the Ending as it presently exists and then report to the Publisher. You will then be allocated there a new Down-Load for the Sequel of your choice. We apologise for any inconvenience caused.

Should the Sequel be delayed so long that you run the risk of falling asleep, please contact the Service Desk to be allocated a Couch. We apologise for any inconvenience.

We regret that Footnotes cannot be reimbursed. This is because the Proof-Reading was performed by an Outside Agency.

Thank you for Reading this Story today. We apologise for any inconvenience caused and we hope you will enjoy the read and we look forward to your reading our Books again.

MORAL:- Better start with Volume 2 first, just in case.

****

No. 444 THE READER SURVEY

Now that you have read this Story, we ask you please to take five minutes and complete the Customer Satisfaction Survey.

Please circle a number: –

1 for 'Not very', 2 for 'Not', 3 for 'No Opinion', 4 for 'Very', 5 for 'Very much".

Did you enjoy the Plot?
1   2   3   4   5

Were   the   Descriptions   adequate?
1   2   3   4   5

What did you make of the Characterisation of the Hero / Heroine / Villain ?
  Was it well-rounded with adequate depth and personal information?   1   2   3   4   5

Could the Story have done with more Sub-Plots?
                1   2   3   4   5

Was there adequate Romantic Interest?
1   2   3   4   5

Were the Sex scenes realistic?*
1   2   3   4   5

Did the Story meet your expectations?
1   2   3   4   5

Would you read another Story from this Author?
                1   2   3   4   5

Would you recommend this Author to your friends (if you have any)?   1   2   3   4   5

Press here:

****

SUBMIT

****

Thank you for taking the time to complete this Reader Survey. Your name will now be entered into a Directory and you will constantly and repeatedly be sent details of many other Offers, whether you want them or not.

MORAL:-   Can you respond without being irresponsible?

****

* How do you know?

No. 445 AUTOMATION

Automated Stories are now all the rage, to the rage and outrage of experienced Readers. They are presented and marketed as Audio Books or as electronic downloads onto Tablets (though not clay tablets). To make our Stories up to date we have introduced this method too.

The idea is very simple. In order to prevent the Reader from having to exercise his or her eyes and brain, and run thereby the risk of straining the nerves linking them, the effort of Reading is removed. The text is presented (rather than 'read') by an automated voice. This also means that any chance of the Imagination being switched in and creating unfortunate memories is also reduced, thus almost eliminating both alarming nightmares or erotic fantasies. One can listen to the texts or 'Stories' through headphones, for privacy, or the loudspeaker attachment of most Smartphones, Tablets and i-Pads.

We present here an example in the hope that this technique will attract you and save you further physical and mental (not to mention emotional or imaginational) effort.

Press the Button for Automatic Story Play.

▶

Should you encounter problems, go to <ohheckwhatisup.com> and follow the link to 'Problem Resolution' and then click on one of the fourteen possible fields. These should lead you to relevant articles which you may Download. If there are problems with the Downloading, contact your service provider through the INTP, NITP, PITN or PINT portals.

If necessary, you may download a hard printed copy of the Story Text from a Bookstore.

We wish you happy listening!

MORAL:- Happiness is not automatic. Everything else can be dealt with digitally.

****

No. 446 STRESS

Oh my God I am so stressed! I have a deadline I need to reach to the end of this page within three and a half minutes and I really don't know how I am going to manage it because I have SO many other things to do and to think about at the same time! There is the shopping and the laundry and I don't know what we are going to do about dinner tonight and who will be home for it and whether everyone will be able to come home on time and what should I do if anyone is late? Do we have enough wine in the house? Is the living room tidy enough and has anyone cleaned the kitchen this week? How am I meant to concentrate on writing this story if I have all these other worries plaguing me at the same time? Oh, it's all too much, too much happening all at the same time! Why does everything have to happen at once? It is so unfair, and it is always happening to ME! There is never any time to stop and think for a moment about all the other things one has to do in order to keep up with all the demands that modern life places upon us. If I am going to write this story I need some space, some peace, I need to be able to sit back calmly for a while and to think a bit about what it is I want to write, how I could best express it, to think of a good opening sentence, something that will really get the whole story into a bit of a swing and carry the reader through into the next paragraph if possible. These things don't just happen by themselves, you know, you need time to polish the idea and form it and put it down Just Right and right now I don't seem to have the time to do this properly at all! How on earth am I going to get down to it? The cleaning lady hasn't come and the post I was expecting hasn't arrived yet and it should have come yesterday if not the day before, really, one cannot rely upon ANYONE these days, not even the post! Heavens I seem to be almost halfway down the page and I haven't even started the Story yet, but I cannot think of anything right now, my mind is so full of all kinds of other things, distractions, how can anyone write anything sensible at all under these conditions?

Now then. Pause, close your eyes, think, think, THINK! Soon this will all be past and maybe then I can concentrate better and get something written, I think I still have a minute and a half or so and if I can only concentrate then maybe I will be able to manage something after all. Mustn't panic, no, MUSTN'T PANIC! Just thinking about it gets me stressed though, I feel breathless and my head is pounding and my back aches and my neck too, all my joints seem to be protesting because of the strain my body is under right now, but I just need to focus properly and then things will be all right, I am sure of that, people always say so, but then again, what do other people know of the stress I am under? Bloody know-it-alls, they are always full of gratuitous advice but has any of them ever had to go through what I have to go through, eh? Just what you need, is people coming and giving you advice you haven't asked for and don't need and that totally overlooks the reality of the situation. But the world is full of people like that and they get in the way and interrupt you and hold you back from doing what you have to do and – did I mention money troubles? The tax demand that came yesterday and that letter from the bank lying on the table and the school fees will be due next month again and I really don't know how we are going to afford a holiday at all this year, the way prices are going and there's another fare increase on the way they say, it just never stops, electricity, gas, the council tax, the kids will need new shoes again soon and somehow people expect me to cope with all of this and not let it get to me and write nice happy stories on time for the deadline - oh my god the deadline - how long do I still have left? Only another thirty seconds or so and my head is still full of all these distractions and I can feel my heart pounding, my pulse feels high, this cannot be good for me, but if I don't write SOMETHING in time then I may as well give up – oh for heaven's sake let's just write something and hope it will flow from there, so, Once upon a time there was, there was, what the hell was there? There must have been something, there always is, oh heavens........I am so stressed....

MORAL:- Take a deep breath! It could be your last one...................

No. 447 BEST BEFORE

It sometimes happens that you open an old book and find in it a story that is really well past its best date. (Books have 'Sell by' Dates because the booksellers wish to make a profit before the remainder get remaindered, but Stories have an existence of their own.)

This is an ancient question: How old does a book have to be before it becomes simply Out of Date? For many Christians, large parts of the Hebrew Bible fall into this category. They call it 'Old'. They only focus upon the few bits that seem to match the ending they already have in mind. And even within the Bible there are many references to other books which have simply been discarded over the centuries. Especially when each book needed to be copied manually and weighed an enormous amount, there had to be a really good incentive to keep a text in circulation! Occasional archaeological discoveries in ancient storerooms in synagogues or monasteries (or caves near the Dead Sea) show us how many books were simply left to decay unread for centuries, no longer needed, no longer relevant. No longer 'modern'.

History books change because History changes. For example: A History Book of Germany may have been published in the Kaiser's time, in the Weimar Republic time, in the National Socialist time, the War time, the Cold War time, it may have been published in what was the DDR or it may have been published after the Reunification. In each case the history it describes and the way it describes it will be totally different. More to the point, if in the Weimar time you still had a book published describing German history from the Kaiser's viewpoint, glorifying the Colonies in Africa and criticising other European nations such as France or Denmark, you were a dangerous Recidivist, Irredentist and Monarchist;

If in the Nazi time you had one which criticised War and stressed the basis of German democracy or maybe of the common values of workers around the world, you would be perceived as a dangerous Enemy of the People, maybe a Communist; If in the 1950's you still clung to your books which had swastikas on the covers and pictures of a certain Adolf, describing Germany's mission to overcome inferior races and acquire 'Lebensraum', you were a dangerous hidden Nazi (like a hidden Sabbataean but more modern). If in the DDR you had a book which had been published in the West you were a 'Staatsfeind' because you possessed and read literature demonstrating a different viewpoint. If, in the late 1990's, you were still quoting from books published in the DDR then you were Unreconstructed and demonstrated a nostalgic view for a totalitarian society. And so on. We don't yet know what the next phase may be – perhaps a future generation of European children will have to learn their history from books which take their viewpoint from China, rather than the other way around.

But we can see how it is sometimes necessary to throw away books which have passed their 'Use By' date, which have become unreadable and indigestible, rotten to the core, through the passage of time. At the very least the paper can be pulped and recycled. Try this:

"Yea!" quoth the Prince, "Thou traitorous Varmint! And ye! How be it, ye knaves and rapscallions! Have at ye, or by God I shall take your gizzards and slit them!"

You find that the language has become old-fashioned, the spellings and vocabulary antiquated. It is hard for the modern reader to enjoy. Tastes have changed. No-one says or writes "Thou" any more. Throw it away.

Then there are issues of political correctness. Consider this example:

"She felt his hot breath on her skin as he ripped the thin silk shift from her shoulders, his hands reaching out to encompass the glowing moistened globes of her breasts as she panted in excitement waiting urgently for him to possess her......."

There are some who would describe this not as 'erotic' but as 'sexist', for clearly there is a dominant heterosexual male here and the act of love is described in terms merely of 'possession'.

But what about:

"You're a fucking poofter, a shirt-lifter, you bastard!" cried Johnny as his schoolmaster hastily withdrew his hand from inside the young lad's shorts. "I'll tell everyone about this! Unless of course...." Johnny looked thoughtfully at the terrified eyes in the sweating face of his Latin teacher, "Unless you give me head, now, and I mean good head, OK?"

There are some who would wince at the homophobic and paedophilic undertones in this passage and declare it unfit for modern consumption. Likewise ancient stories which feature negro slaves in anything but an heroic role are considered unfit for school use.

This is why modern novels always carry a label which makes it clear that they are:

"Best before:
END.

MORAL:- Some things last longer but nothing lasts forever.

No. 448 FORCE OF GRAVITY

Throughout Life one is subject to Gravity, which is another way of saying that one is constantly on one's way to the Grave – a grave matter, indeed and one to be treated with appropriate gravitas. Sooner or later we must all come down to earth. And be absorbed into it. But it is hardly surprising that one often feels pulled down by forces beyond one's control. There is, unfortunately, no escape from this.

Life is sometimes like walking along the edge of a cliff. One has the feeling that at any moment <u>one could stumble and f</u>

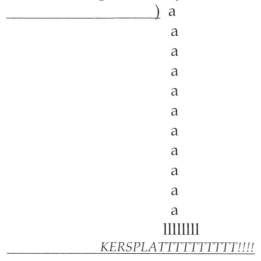

```
                           ) a
                             a
                             a
                             a
                             a
                             a
                             a
                             a
                             a
                             a
                             a
                          lllllll
           KERSPLATTTTTTTTTT!!!!
```

MORAL:-   Keep your balance! No-one has ever yet defeated the Force of Gravity.

****

No. 449 THE SLIPPERY SLOPE

There was once a gentle Slope. He lay calmly and gently like this

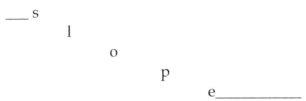

Someone observed him and got very worried. "What would happen if anyone were to fall and roll down you?" he asked.

"Oh, don't worry," replied the Slope slopishly, "I am very gentle and he will come slowly to the bottom and not get hurt."

"But what if you were to get steeper?" asked the Worrier. "Just think, it could rain and you would get wet and then he would slide and slip! It could snow and then the surface could become icy and treacherous. We must DO something about you, before it is too late!"

"But why?" asked the Slope. "I am quite contented the way I am. I have a gentle gradient, I am really one in a thousand. You need have no fear of me, I serve a useful function here, linking two levels some distance apart. Just relax! Stay level-headed and let me incline myself according to my own inclination."

"No, don't you see the danger?" responded the Worrier. Such Worriers always worry about what they call 'slippery slopes', by which they mean that what starts off looking minor and harmless could theoretically change and get steeper and more dangerous and they might lose control. This says more about them and their own powers of braking and self-control than it does about the Slope itself but – well, that's they way things often are. Their arguments are irrational and there is no point in applying a sliding scale to them, because this is exactly what they worry about most. It is so often more sloppy thinking than slopey thinking.

"You might get like this," he said and he demonstrated:
_____Sl
       o
         o
            o
            o
          o
           o
          o
              p
             e _____

"I say, I think that's a bit steep - Don't take the precipice out of me," said the Slope. "I am not a cliff-hanger. I can incline as well as decline, you know. Anyway, since a slope is a matter of degrees, if you de-grease one then it will not be slippery. That's very logical, you know."

The Worrier had however already headed down the slippery slope towards Panic, Hysteria and Paranoia. That can happen if you let go too soon.....

MORAL: Best to stay on the level if you can.

****

117

No. 450 THE DANGER OF BOOKS

Reading can be a surprisingly dangerous occupation. Recently I was so deeply absorbed in a fascinating text that I overran my station again – the problem being that in this case and on this train the next station was some hundred and forty miles further on. One is just, as it were, carried away.

I am reminded of the story of my former colleague Professor Herbert Walsh-Jenkins, who vanished one day. He was, shall we say, somewhat bookish. Well, I say he vanished – in fact what happened was that one of his undergraduate students came at the appointed time for a supervision and found no sign of the Professor in his study. This was surprising, as the Professor had been noted there barely an hour previously when one of the College servants had brought him a tray with tea, teacups and so forth, and he had not been seen to pass the Lodge since that time. The student – not a very assiduous one, it must be remarked at this point – felt rather light-hearted and even relieved about the prospect of missing his weekly supervision with the Professor, for he had not come adequately prepared and had been expecting to have to bluff his way through; But then, after sitting down and eating two of the remaining biscuits on the plate on the tray on the Professor's desk (a Custard Cream and a Ginger Nut, if you must know) he thought he heard a faint call for help and, on tracing the call to its presumed source, found this to be a large and malevolent-looking tome with a dark leather binding lying on the Professor's desk. He opened the book, a little gingerly (maybe having had that Ginger Nut helped in this respect) and there was a sudden loud clap, as of thunder, and suddenly the Professor was there, sitting in his seat and coughing, covered in a thin layer of paper dust.

"Oh dear," he said. "I really lost myself in that book. It was quite strange, as I could not find the way out or even the End. Normally I devour books, but this time the book seemed to absorb <u>me</u> - totally."

The student learned from this experience (at least) and hardly ever opened a book again unless it was filled mainly with brightly-coloured pictures, with the text safely confined to enclosed bubbles. He kept well away from any tome labelled a 'Digest'. (Even after filling himself with digestive biscuits.)

As for Professor Walsh-Jenkins himself, a few years later he wandered into the University Library and has not been seen again. Having long been unofficially considered absent-minded he is now officially classified as 'absent-bodied' as well, which means he has not officially been retired, his Chair has not been re-advertised and his modest stipend continues to be paid into his bank account. Nevertheless, for the last three years, for pragmatic reasons, his lectures have been officially removed from the university calendar. If you ask, you will be told he is suffering from Equi-Librium, and he is classed as '*Ex Libris*'.

MORAL:- Avoid sets of Complete Works and always keep those pages turning! Even a small book can have a large volume.

No. 451   ERROR 613

This message was created automatically. Your Story cannot be read. The Plot you have chosen is unavailable. Check your readership and literary intentions. Code ERROR 613 on xxx.noplot.poorplot.xxx This is a permanent error. There is a Narrative Break and this programme will not run on Onceuponatime. Please check with your Story Provider for new developments or download Plot 2.0. New Characters are necessary and can be downloaded free at www.characters4all.com.

Read the licensing notes on accredited Authorship at

SmallPrintSmallPrintSmallPrintSmallPrintSmallPrintSmallPrintSmallPrintSmallPrintSmallPrintSmall
PrintSmallPrintSmallPrintSmallPrintSmallPrintSmallPrintSmallPrintSmallPrintSmallPrintSmallPrintS
mallPrintSmallPrintSmallPrintSmallPrintSmallPrintSmallPrintSmallPrintSmallPrintSmallPrintSmallPr
intSmallPrintSmallPrintSmallPrintSmallPrintSmallPrintSmallPrintSmallPrintSmallPrintSmallPrintSm
allPrintSmallPrintSmallPrintSmallPrintSmallPrintSmallPrintSmallPrintSmallPrintSmallPrintSmallPrin
tSmallPrintSmallPrintSmallPrintSmallPrintSmallPrintSmallPrintSmallPrintSmallPrintSmallPrintSmall
PrintSmallPrintSmallPrintSmallPrintSmallPrintSmallPrintSmallPrintSmallPrintSmallPrintSmallPrintS
mallPrintSmallPrintSmallPrintSmallPrintSmallPrintSmallPrintSmallPrintSmallPrintSmallPrintSmallPr
intSmallPrintSmallPrintSmallPrintSmallPrintSmallPrintSmallPrint

and tick the box to confirm agreement. [ ]

Host FairyTales.com cannot connect to your narrative. Check all Fiction connections. If necessary, Access your Server at Inspiration.org or Creativity.ac.ade for new Openings.

The wait for a new Paragraph has exceeded the Maximum Waiting Period. No new Paragraph can now be inserted. Discard and begin again.

Check your Port is connected to Starboard or Storyboard. Any older Ports should be decanted.

MORAL:- To Reboot is an Attribute or a Retribute.

****

Walter Rothschild. Version 17.04.2017

No. 452 PRELIMINARIES

Dear Readers,

Welcome to this Volume of Stories. My name is Walter Rothschild and I am your Author for this Story. In the name of my Editor and Publisher I welcome you to this Literary Experience. We hope you will enjoy a pleasant reading. We shall begin shortly with the opening sentences. Thank you for choosing This Story today. Our estimated Reading Time is 4 minutes and 30 seconds. We shall read at the heights of fantasy and descend to the depths of tragic emotion.

Members of our Frequent Readers Scheme will get ten points for completing this story. If you are interested in joining our Frequent Readers Scheme, speak to your local Librarian. We have many other volumes available for your future pleasure, just ask for details.

Should you need to interrupt the story part-way for any reason, to take refreshments or to meet natural needs, please mark the page and close the book immediately. Bookmarks will be made available. If you are reading to a child, explain the need for the break BEFORE marking the page and closing the book. Do not pick up any other books in the meantime as this will interrupt the flow. Should the lights go out, we advise you to cease reading until full visibility is restored.

We are now about to commence. Please put down all teacups or wine glasses and stow them away carefully to avoid spillage; Ensure hands are clean, check your cushions and lean back in your seats. We wish you an enjoyable read.

"Once upon a time........"

MORAL:- Sometimes, to enjoy a good book you really do need to have your head in the clouds.

****

No. 453 THE PERFECT MURDER

It was, truly, the perfect murder. The one all murderers and potential murderers dream about. Everyone knew that it had happened, but no-one knew much more. There was no corpse that had been found, there were no witnesses. No-one was sure exactly where and when the murder had been committed, nor even how, let alone by whom or why. The victim – for there must have been one, at least one – was unknown.

The only trouble was, from the point of view of the author or authoress of criminal novels and detective thrillers, that there was nothing to write. There was no motive to analyse, no means to describe. There were neither main nor subsidiary characters. If there is no plot that can be discerned, how can one manage to weave a sub-plot into the narrative construction? There is no corpse that can be described in all its gory detail as it is discovered. No-one even knows whether it is worth calling in a Police Inspector to interview all the potential witnesses and suspects, for there was nothing to witness and no-one knows whom to suspect.

So, a general air of puzzled helplessness spread. The 'Orient Express' departed, and arrived, without incident and with a full complement of passengers. On the Nile the only death reported was that of a tourist who inadvertently swallowed some of the water and suffered in consequence a swift and fatal but wholly-explicable attack of typhoid. No corpse cluttered the Library at the Grand House. No dismembered body parts lay and rotted in plastic bags in obscure alleyways. No remembered insults were paid off with strychnine. There seemed to be no weapon to be searched for and, when found, identified. In short, Inspector Morose who had, for form's sake, been called in and had been instructed to make whatever investigations he could, had given up in frustration and despair and had gone off to listen to an opera. Lewis was left looking into his half-emptied half-pint glass while Miss Marple's tea pot grew cold and Sherlock's pipe smouldered down to nothingness. Murder most foul? More of a foul-up.

Oh well. Let us hope there is more to report in the next such bout of criminal activity.

MORAL:- One can indeed kill off an entire literary genre.

****

No. 454 'EALTH AN' SAFETY

Before you start this Story: STOP! CHECK! Do you know where the End is, should you need to access it in an Emergency?

What is your **Safety Case** for this Story? CHECK: Do you know: Who wrote it?

Who published it?

Who printed it, and where?

Is the Paper acid-free?

What is the chemical composition of the (a) Ink and (b) Glue?

Are there any contra-indications in terms of mixture or inflammability?

Who laid out the individual Pages?

Is the binding stiff?

Do you have clear Information: How much it cost? What **Insurance** Policies apply to this Work? Do you have all relevant telephone numbers and a **First Aid** Team with fully-equipped and checked equipment to hand?

Some Stories contain **Excitement** or even **Erotic Arousal**. Check that 5 Buckets of Cold Water are available within ten metres. Children and Persons of a Weak Disposition (PWD) should be kept at least two metres from the Book until its content has been checked by a competent and qualified Adult Reader.

Eye Protection – Reading can cause painful Eyestrain. Ensure that Eyes are protected against Dust, Sharp Objects and Glare. Is the Light adequate for reading? Is the lamp properly adjusted? Check published **Regulations for Ocular Protection**.

Fingertip Protection – the edges of paper pages can be sharp. Do you have adequate fingertip protection provided? Also tissues, cotton wool, disinfectant in liquid or ointment form and plasters?

What is the estimated **Reading Time**? Have arrangements been put in place for Comfort Breaks every Ten Minutes? **Refreshments** (Non-alcoholic) should be prepared in advance in case a Snack is required part-way through.

When all the above have been checked and re-checked and the application approved by a qualified Literary Health and Safety Adviser, and the Application of Story Reading (form NAR/21/c) has been signed and stamped Here:

and
Here:..(Date):..
......

you may begin to read the Story. Happy Reading!

MORAL:- There may be Safety in Numbers but Words can be Dangerous, as every tyrant knows.

****

No. 455 SPECIAL FEATURE!!
THE TEN BEST-KEPT SECRETS!!

1. A Royal Personage suffers from a specific complaint. However, we do not know what the nature of this complaint is, nor the name of the Royal Personage, nor indeed the name of the country which he or she rules.

2. A certain thespian performer of theatrical entertainments, an actor of both stage and film, has for some time pursued a romantic liaison with another young (female) thespian, although he is at present officially married. The name of this thespian is however unknown, as is the extent to which this romantic liaison has gone.

3. The best-kept secret location for a really wonderful, peaceful and above all affordable Holiday is ...... still a secret.

4. The best way to make a large amount of money very quickly and totally legally (at least in some countries which are well known as havens for such activities) is to – We cannot say.

5. Behind the text of the Holy Bible is, according to many theologians, a secret unholy version which has been overwritten. The secrets of this invisible but putative work (the Mystic or Secret Codex) have yet to be deciphered or interpreted. Even the initiated and illuminated are still ignorant of its content or importance or even existence.

6. What does the Pope dream about? He refuses to tell anyone.

7. The planet Earth has a specific and limited life-span. The Globe is due to collapse inwards upon itself in a certain number of centuries. The exact number is known only to those who have understood the secret prophecies of VostraDummus – but they keep this secret to themselves.

8. The most recent Presidential Elections were notable for the number of voters who cast their vote logarithmically, thus ensuring that any majority had to be a factor of *Pi*. How they managed to calculate this is unknown.

9. A Lady's secrets should always be kept discreetly secret, or else she is no Lady, only a Secretary.

10. It is very easy for a Man to make a Woman happy. He must merely find out what it is she really wants. But – What is this? No-one can yet say.

MORAL:- Discretion is an important part of Morality. The secret is that it is best to keep secret secretions secret.

****

No. 456 ADVICE TO A TRAPPIST NOVICE

MORAL:- Don't say you were not warned. In fact, Don't say Anything.

****

(Shush!)

No. 457 JINGLE BOOKS

Welcome to Classic Lit.! At Classic Lit we bring you all the quotes you need for a really fun day. (Jingle – *Classic Lit! A lotta Lit!*) I am Jeff Boreham and I'll be with you till the end of Chapter Four.

Here is a bit from a famous novel by one of England's greatest writers, Charles Dickens, read for us by Henry Longbottom from the Penguin edition:

"It was the best of times, it was the worst of times." Yes, well, that may be so, but it is all we have time for right now as I have this really super passage just waiting to be read!

Jane Austen was one of the best-known women authors of the eighteenth century, here from the Everyman edition, the opening sentences:

"It is a fact undisputed that a young man in possession of two hundred pounds a year...."

(Jingle – *Classic LIT for YOU!!!*)

One of the greatest stars of the Elizabethan age, a real leader in the dramatic scene of the time, was Will Shakespeare, often referred to as William. He wrote lots and lots of plays, some of which are still played regularly even today. Here is an excerpt from his Race drama Othello, which has such a lot to say even today about attitudes to racism and sexism:

"Reputation, Reputation, Reputation. Who steals my purse steals trash, 'twas mine, 'tis his, and now 'tis nothing worth. But he who steals from me mine own good name, takes that which riches him but not at all, yet leaves me poor indeed..."

Some interesting thoughts there, I think. I do so prefer this speech to the "Out, vile jelly!" scene when this other guy gets his eyes pushed out. Not nice. Makes you wonder a bit about Shakespeare. Not really one for the kids. Not Lite-Lit. Best stick to Winnie the Pooh, I reckon, and Honey not Jelly!

(Jingle – *Classic* – *LIT!!*)

Now here's a rather unusual piece, not at all well known, I think it is fair to say; One of our listeners has asked for it specially. It's actually a translation of a little-known work by the obscure Finnish writer Helöööö Guddbaiij – I looked him up on the internet and learned that not a löt is really known about him but this piece really inspired several other Finnish writers in the 1880's to, as one might say, finnish the jobs they were working on. The translation is by Ooo Paijjama and the book is published by Camera Obscura of Luton: Here it is read to us, by Pete Sake, in the translation by Dickson Herry. I've taken the whole of the Second Chapter.

"The night sky was still black. It was, if anything, even blacker than the evening sky had been, earlier, as he had begun this contemplation in his black mood. The stars were small pieces of brightness, infinitesimally small, within the dark blackness of the black dark sky. In the dark woods Riiiisto looked around him, wondering, again, whether it was really worth the effort of opening his eyes, or blinking. The black wind blew blackly against his face and he knew that this would continue steadily until at least the end of April, when the light winds would begin and blow steadily against his back until the end of September when the black winds would resume once more. Unless, of course, he were to turn around. But this would change everything, for then the front would become the back and the back would become the front, until – and only then – he decided to turn back once more, to resume his original direction. One needs a sense of direction, he thought, to make any sense at all out of these black nights with the black wind blowing blackly and bleakly through the black woods. Was it all a metaphor for the soul, deprived of the warm redness of the wood-lined sauna and the dry hot billows of overheated steam? No, maybe not. That would be too easy and, if there was one thing of which he was certain, totally certain, absolutely certain, certainly certain, it was that such easy responses and metaphors had no place in a work as dark and black as this. Let April come and then, perhaps, he could decide.

But how would he know when April came? The thought caught hold of the shreds of his dark soul. Would it be when the light winds began? Or would it be when, against his initial decision, he turned round after all? Could he make April come earlier, could he hold it back to make it come later? There was, he knew, no way in which he could blow the winds back again. He huddled deeper into his black parka coat and stood, thinking."

Wow, that is such an _amazing_ Second Chapter! It sort of moves you while letting you stand still, if you know what I mean.

Well, the News is coming soon – with all the latest news from our LitCrit Newsroom on the next Book Fairs, forthcoming book launches and publications. We will also have more on the dispute between the Society of Authors and the Government on tax implications of the proposed Pay-By-The-Word scheme and how it would affect minimalist Poets.

(Jingle – _Classic Lit! A book every day!_)

- And later this evening: Hardbacks for Beginners. Also Part Fourteen of our weekly Guide to Non-Fiction. Thank you for choosing Classic Lit. today! And Happy Reading!

(Jingle – _"Get Lit Up!"_)

"Advertising. "P-p-p-p-p-ick up a Penguin, or a P-Puffin, or a P-Pelican.... But don't forget to Pay! Book a Book Now!"

"Book Club of the Month – can YOU afford not to be a member? Join Now!! Details on Owe-Won-Three-Five-Won-Owe-Too-Four-Ate or under dubbelyoo-dubbelyoo-trebbelyoo-dot-booksforall.com."

(Jingle – _Classic Lit – The News for You!_)

MORAL:- Commercial literary stations just don't have time for morals. Leave that to the BBC.

****

No. 458 THE GHOST WRITER

Many so-called celebrities and others who are insufficiently literate and inadequately trained, employ what they term as 'Ghost Writers' to compose books which are sold as 'Autobiographies'. There are Sportsmen whose main skills lie in running fast up and down a field, or so-called celebrities who are famous because they have appeared several times playing somebody else on the television screen, even minor politicians, or persons who think that others would be interested in reading about their (modest) contribution to society, immodestly presented in a thick hard-back book with an illustrated dust jacket just in time for the Xmas market......... But in fact, this is an incorrect term; it describes an enslaved hack, one who makes his meagre living and earns his crust by doing the hard work for someone else and placing the results in the first person singular. Often such books bear a title saying something like "My Life" whereas what they really mean is "My Life – until Now." These poor scriveners are authors without authority, writers without rights; they let dictators dictate to them and they have to make a better job of the content than the dictator usually managed himself. Unable to get a life for themselves, they write the lives of others. The end result is of course often a tactful hybrid of Fact and Fiction.

Real Ghost Writers though are different and rarely get to see any hard copy of their work. But records have to be completed, wherever one may be and in whichever dimension. No-one likes an unfinished story that trails off at just the point where it should begin to get exciting. And so, one has Ghost Writers. These are the scribes who take over AFTER the deadline, so to speak.

Once you get used to the properties of ectoplasm it isn't so hard to make notes. But there is a sort of living to be made, if that is not the wrong term, from writing the Final Chapter for people's autobiographies – the chapters they never get around to writing themselves, for obvious reasons.

Nevertheless, this can be a tricky job. Some of the authors are quite bitter about the way their life stories were ended well before they were expecting; some had envisaged further volumes of speeches or sermons or deeds of heroism and were very disappointed when their corpus was prematurely completed through their becoming themselves a corpse. In such case a relatively brief chapter should as far as possible stay factual, on the lines of :

> "I was not really expecting the bullet that came out of the ambush. Leading my unit, I had expected to take the enemy position without too much trouble and without too many casualties – at least on our side – and was even privately hoping for another Bar to my DSO as a consequence – that would be one up on that damned arrogant Lieutenant Smithers of the 3rd. Battalion, who didn't even have one Bar yet and had never even been Mentioned in Despatches! Never had I considered that I myself might become one of the casualties...."

and so on.

Even these endings are relatively easy compared to:

> "I shall never forgive my bastard of a brother for the way he stuck the dagger in my back as I stood at the top of the staircase. Talk about Cain and Abel! Or brotherly love! Sibling rivalry had reached its extreme, for he had never forgiven me for the sin of having emerged into the world those few seconds before he. The wretched traitor acted as though he were going to greet me, to slap me on the shoulder, when suddenly I felt the burning sensation inside my body as the blade struck home. I was almost too astonished to feel the brief but intense pain before my consciousness was so abruptly terminated."

Then you have those embarrassing situations where, as ghost biographer, you need to be really, really certain that the subject of your book really wants potentially embarrassing issues to be raised at all. Many would rather have them as discreetly covered as they themselves have been. What should one write in such a situation?

"I had not expected her wretched husband to return home so early. Sheila, who for obvious reasons had a better view of the bedroom door opening than did I at that moment, screamed and made me aware that there was something wrong, for this was not her normal squeal of ecstatic delight at such moments. I turned round, twisting my spine quite painfully as I did so, being as I was caught up in complex and mutual physical exertions. The fellow looked exceedingly irate but, well, I have dealt with many a cuckolded husband in my time. Besides, I too had good reason for annoyance at this sudden and rather brutal, undignified form of interruptus. Nevertheless, I confess I was quite taken aback, so much so that I delayed a few fatal moments before springing out of the bed and reaching for my pistol which was, of course, still in its holster attached to the belt in my trousers. But too late! ...."

Or:

"He came towards me and reached out with both hands – I thought he would embrace me, forgive me, pull me close to him and shower me with kisses and tears, and all would be well again. But no! Suddenly his hands were round my neck, his thumbs pushing deep into my throat, the windpipe, blocking the air from my mouth and nose, from my lungs – I felt blackness all around me, I saw stars flashing, I felt the world around me grow hazier and more distant, I was trying to scream but could not, instead I felt only his thumbs pushing so hard and I saw the expression on his face, an expression not only of anger but of hatred, and I knew then that all was lost. To say that I was breathless with amazement would be an understatement, but breathless I was. With one final attempt at a gasp, at a sigh of regret, I let go and allowed myself to float as my body fell crumpled to the floor...."

Another example from the current crop of releases:

"Looking back, perhaps that sixth double vodka was a mistake. I admit this fully now, because I regret still the damage caused to my so-perfect and so lovingly maintained and polished Daimler which, I am reliably informed, needed to be scrapped later. But the call of the open road was irresistible, the wonderful exhilarating feeling of the trees flashing past as I put my foot down on the pedal – I suppose this is how Mister Toad must have felt in his open-topped sports car and for a moment my mind flashed back to Nanny reading me the story of 'Wind in the Willows' as a boy before she expertly masturbated me again, "to help me sleep" as she always said. Personally, I always thought she just liked the taste and once I rather naughtily used some of Father's shaving foam rather than the normal Nursery perfumed soap, but she was unfazed and merely said I got more like my father every day. It was while I was basking in these warm childhood memories that my hand must have lost its grip on the steering wheel for suddenly there was a tree coming swiftly towards me – I realise that, according to normal natural laws, I must have been approaching the tree swiftly and not the other way round but, in such moments, there is little time for rational cogitation. What would Nanny say now, I wonder, if she were to learn that it was thinking back to her tender ministrations that led me indeed into this 'Big Sleep'?"

Many a person likes to boast of their life, but few are quite so proud of their demise. Further, although many of those who require ghost writers to complete the accounts of their abruptly-ended reigns are Royal, there are few royalties paid. And although many writers would love to achieve immortality, there is little one can do when writing about it. But at least the Ghost Writers have the satisfaction of being able to type 'The End' – and mean it.

MORAL:- There are few REALLY happy endings. And no-one likes to be written-off.

****

Walter Rothschild who-ooh-ooooh……

No. 459 THE SPLIT INFINITIVE

There was once a Spit Infinitive. He could no longer recall how he had been split, but he was quite bitter about it – two bits, in fact. "Infinity is a Continuum," he said, "it <u>has</u> to be, by definition, and when you split it you have only two semi-finite temporal entities – one beginning somewhere in the infinite past but ending in the here-and-now present, one commencing in the here-and-now but extending indefinitely into the future" – he was most definite about that but the point is, to be indefinite is definitely not the same as being infinite. It was pathetic, really. One could not even tell which bit was longer, as both were immeasurable.

Should he now be 'In-finitive'? Or 'Infin-itive'? 'Infiniti-ve'? Where should the split best be placed? It is not fair to always split an Infinitive but then provide no guidance on the hypothetical hyphenation.

In vain was it pointed out to him that those who seek to go to "Infinity – and Beyond!" did need at least a starting-point for their endeavours. "I want to always compare this with – Oh damn, I have split myself again!" he exclaimed. In fact, this was a surprisingly common occurrence – surprising at least to those who always wish to be repeatedly surprised. Since an Infinite Length must, by its own definition, have neither Beginning nor End and yet not necessarily form an endless circular pattern, then any splits have to always be internal ones; one cannot say, for example, that the Infinitive had to always split itself from another Infinitive – oh bugger, it's happened again – for example a parallel one – with which it had run together but alongside – and it is indeed a long side when each is infinite. So the internal split divides eternal conceptions to not make them immaculate; Leaving a maculature of SEMI-infinite length, an utter contradiction in terms. Can you begin to sensitively understand how the imposition of an Adverb into the middle of an Infinitive splits it more effectively than an atom? On the other hand, there are those theologians who claim that only if you split – say, One into Three - can you begin to finally understand splituality. But - Beware of theologians who can turn an exquisite faith into an Inquisition and divide Infinity into Exfinities with extremism at the extremes.

This Split Infinitive began to actively consider what could be done to quickly repair the breach before it could begin to dangerously duplicate itself, creating a pair of breaches. Things looked black and as is well known black breeches can, when torn, produce black holes into which all matter must fall. Each leg in the breeches might begin to divergently go its own way, each seeking its own legitimation.

The only hope is if some verbal form begins to glue in the dark, for then one can attempt to carefully glue the sections together again in an attempt to possibly restore Infinity, at least insofar as one can measure it, which of course one cannot, thus creating a new but at least different set of mathematical unquantifiable quantum problems.

This produces a new form of extended, suspended, up-ended but not-to-be-ended Infinity which is viable and even justifiable but at the same time liable to carelessly split all over again – thus leading to a repetitive competitive issue and a new cycle of 'doing the splits'. For some, this can be infinitely boring.

And so on, *ad infinitum*.....

MORAL:- It's rude to split!

****

No. 460 A BORING LOVE STORY

Once upon a time there was a young man who fell in love with a beautiful young girl who lived in the same town. At the same time, she fell deeply in love with him. She was his very first girl friend and he was her first boy friend. Her parents approved of him and his parents were very happy about her for, after all, they all belonged to the same church and lived in the same suburb in very similar houses. And so a wedding was organised, not too quiet but not too extravagant. All the guests who were invited came to the celebration and no-one was missed out by mistake. The young couple moved into a flat of their own and really, really enjoyed their married life together and raised a happy family of healthy, bonny and loving children.

MORAL:- Well, it's pretty hard to make a dramatic Opera out of something like that, isn't it?

****

No. 461 THE SCIENCE OF READING

Notice:- This Story has been declared an 'SSSI' – A 'Site of Special Scientific Interest'. In consequence we are limited in the number of sentences and paragraphs we may provide at once. This Site has been recognised as a habitat for a rare species of Bookworm, '*anobium punctatum, helluo librorum protolibrensis*', Readers who still prefer to consume paper and ink rather than the more common predatory Facebookers, Bloggers, Twitterers and Whatsappologists. Bookworms prefer Unsocial or even Antisocial Media, their favoured habitat being curled up in a deep armchair.

The relevant authorities	have asked us to
maintain a gap in the	middle of the page to allow
the Bookworms to gain	access to their reading grounds.

Both male and female	Bookworms are characterised
by thick spectacles and a	pale complexion but they make
up for this by an	enhanced fantasy life and a
good inner pictorial ability,	combined with a deepened
memory and an expanded	vocabulary.

By leaving spaces also at	the sides of the page they are
enabled to speed-read their	way to the end of the page if
necessary.	In order to avoid overloading
with words and paragraphs	this Story must now be
brought to a provisional End.	Otherwise the Bookworms
could become overfilled	and have difficulty digesting.

We must do all we can to	save this endangered species
from further diminution	and encourage them to stay
active and read here in	our culture.

MORAL:- Reading is a Science, not an Art. Hence one needs Special Interests.

****

No. 462 THERAPEUTIC READING

It is well known that Reading is a calming experience. It is wonderful to sit in an easy chair, on a window bench, in a hammock, in bed, on a park bench, heavens, even in a moving train and peruse a work of literature. Its effect on the mind, on the nerves is extended through the eyes to the nerve cells and the receptors in the brain. This is why many doctors recommend Reading as a means of overcoming many of the daily stresses of life – albeit, many will warn you that Reading should <u>not</u> be undertaken at the same time as one is actually driving a car, flying an aeroplane; or operating complex machinery. This is a surprisingly common misunderstanding, though one that rarely lasts for very long.

We at the Aesopologetic Foibles Therapeutic Centre have therefore prepared for You, our valued client, this especially soothing piece of Literature.

Start here:

Slo-o-o-o-o-o-w-w-l-l-y. Br-e-e-e-a-a-t-h-e-i-n-n-n..... and n-o-o-w... b-r-e-e-e-e-a-a-t-h-e-o-o-o-o—u-t-t!! My heavens! Already this feels better.

Now start the following sentence, but slowly. This is not an exercise in speed-reading.

Sheila felt the need to sleep, she was so deeply sleepy she could just keep her eyes open.

Read it again, at half the speed as last time.

Now **Yawn**. This is quite easy, even if you were not feeling so tired a few minutes ago. Breathe in deeply and let the breath out through an open mouth, letting whatever sound may come simply come with it, do not try to suppress the sound.

Repeat.

Now breathe deeply. Wasn't that good? Do you think you could cope with another sentence now? Gently does it!

The dreams came gently, slowly, creeping oh so slowly into her mind as she sank deeply into her peaceful sleep...

Mmmmmmmmmmmmmmmmmmmmmmmmmmmmmmmmmm.............
....

<u>MORAL</u>:- Don't turn the page, let the page turn you!

****

No. 463 A BUSY BUSSY BUSINESS STORY

You know, a Story can be very like a Bus. What do I mean? Well, just think about a Bus; Many people share it at the same time, all going in the same direction. They know they would not get there unless there was someone at the front making sure that the bus made progress, safely but determinedly, and followed its path and its schedule, according to the structures laid down for it. In the same way many people can read or hear a Story at the same time, so long as someone is writing it down or reading it aloud to them. Of course, there are many buses and they all go in different directions at different times but you, as the reader, have the choice of which one best suits your needs. Naturally, one has to pay a certain small amount to ride the bus, just as one ought to purchase a book rather than just borrowing it – which brings the author no financial benefit whatsoever.

Some buses are single-deckers and some are double-deckers, which means – just as with stories - there is an extra layer of meaning for those who can reach it. Some are urban, short-distance, just like short stories, for hopping in and out as the fancy or the need takes you, and some go for longer distances, even internationally – just like a good thriller or road novel, for which you need to plan time, such as a long journey or a period in a waiting room. There are pauses along the way, the stages just like new chapters. Some are comfortable and one can relax, in others one feels the closeness to other people and their experiences – or they are simply, like best-sellers, in heavy demand and it can even be that you fail to get one when you want to. They can have colourful exteriors and short texts telling you what you need to know.

And then, sometimes..... well,.... you wait a long time for a suitable story to turn up, a long, long time.... a frustrating time.... an empty time... a time filled with boredom rather than pleasure...... and then.... and then...

…..

…..

…..

…..

TWO identical Stories come at the same time!

Each one filled with promise, indicating that a thrilling journey awaits the happy reader who simply has to get into it, past the opening, and then all will be revealed, although of course all will NOT be revealed until it gets to the end, the terminus, the point of no return - unless you buy another ticket and head all the way back again to start again. Each filled with interesting characters, some mysterious, many with baggage of one sort or another – loners, lovers, families, crowds of the young, the pensive elderly, each at their pace, a truly fascinating mix, and you know it will take you to new, strange places and an unknown destiny........

Each one filled with promise, indicating that a thrilling journey awaits the happy reader who simply has to get into it, past the opening, and then all will be revealed, although of course all will NOT be revealed until it gets to the end, the terminus, the point of no return - unless you buy another ticket and head all the way back again to start again. Each filled with interesting characters, some mysterious, many with baggage of one sort or another – loners, lovers, families, crowds of the young, the pensive elderly, each at their pace, a truly fascinating mix, and you know it will take you to new, strange places and an unknown destiny........

When this happens, do not panic. Just as you cannot get into two buses at the same time, you cannot read two stories at the same time. Or even two pages at the same time (or two sides of the same page). Just immerse yourself into the first one unless it seems overfilled with metaphors and similes, in which case it may be that the second one has more space, more room to feel for yourself. You will still get there in the end.

MORAL:- Hop in quick while you have the chance!

****

No. 464 IT'S TIME!

It was 12.63 and I was beginning to get worried. Time was clearly not standing still, whereas I was. At least, it seemed so. It was, or is, or could be a strange feeling. I had fallen again, I knew, into that shady trench that some call the Fifth Dimension. Time is considered to be the Fourth Dimension but then there is the other Time, the Time that does not just pass, but passes through you, often leaving no trace behind. For example, you may have had the experience of waking with the alarm clock at, say, 6am, and thinking "Good, I still have plenty of time", and then – suddenly – it is 06.23 and one is in a rush, even though one has not slept, read, eaten, bathed or done anything else. It is not as though twenty-three minutes had passed; The Time was simply Not There. Ironically, sometimes this Passing-Through Time leaves no trace of ageing, whereas on other occasions the shock of noticing it has gone by so silently can double the ageing process in time-sensitive individuals and perishable goods.

I waited. I really had little choice, for my appointment was not yet due. The clock ticked but the minute hand was moving faster than the second hand. This is always a slightly disturbing sensation, as when the sun, between mid-February and mid-March, rises in the north-west for reasons no astronomer has ever really managed to understand - and so they pretend it doesn't happen and no-one talks about it. Instead they try to distract us with complications as to how long February is this year, whereas the Chinese refer instead to the Long March - which has 33 days.

Many of my friends and colleagues are slaves to Time, instead of making Time work for them. I feel ambivalent about this, sometimes feeling I need much more time, sometimes wishing it would pass quicker. It sometimes helps to have other interests that run to a different rhythm – it is no coincidence that these are called 'Pastimes'. Sports run to a different seasonal pattern. Sometimes one has Some Times and not just One. This is as chronological as anything else.

But none of this speculation helped now. According to the clock it was now 12.67 and since it showed no sign of pausing, I was being left behind! Would this happen at the End of Time? Could it be that the World would come to an end at a defined and specified and even predicted moment, whilst many of the world's population remained a few days behind, totally unready and unprepared? Anything was possible, anything is possible, anything will be possible, anything will have been or will have become possible once one starts messing about with Time Signatures.

But this is the problem with Time Loops. You usually cannot see them clearly. At first all seems normal and sequential, because there is nothing to which one can compare Time in the other eight dimensions. And then something happens – or might happen or seems to be happening already and continuously and repeatedly and one realises that one dare not even emit, since this is only 'Time' backwards.

While I was pondering this problem, or pondering whether I would ponder it soon, my mobile phone pinged. Here, at least, I thought, was a sign of the Present, something that could bind me to the flow of time in a coherent manner. I looked at it, curious; my friend had sent a text message. "Sorry, I will have been delayed – I can come yesterday instead." Damn! I knew already I would have no free time then. And time that is not free always costs such a lot.

It was now 12.84. Nothing else for it. It was time for tea.

MORAL:- Why stay with just "Once upon a time"? Be more ambitious!

****

146

No. 465 THE LIGHT OF THE CHARGING BRIGADE

Many people think that the growth of modern innovative and digital chip-based technology has freed us from the constraints of time and space - but this is not wholly true. For example, although one can telephone or text someone from almost anywhere, without needing to be standing fixed to a telephone cable which in turn is fixed to a wall and through its network is connected with an Exchange, sooner or later (and usually sooner) the Mobile Telephone itself will need to be plugged by a cable into a power socket or power bank in order to be re-charged. No phone is smart enough to do that by itself. The Laptop may function without a mouse, or with a mouse that is free of any cable, but sooner or later the Laptop or Notebook or Pad or whatever will also need to be re-charged, for nothing lasts forever except human wilfulness and stupidity and naivety. Even 'long life' batteries are as mortal as those who made them, those who buy them and those who use them. If you read an e-Book or a lengthy text that has been sent digitally (i.e. by someone using their digit to press the right buttons and keyboard keys) the power available will gradually reduce over time and the screen lose some of its brightness, even when on a power-saving programme, and the text will gradually fade away and become illeg

What can be done in such cases? We proudly present the first Rechargeable Story. Take your charging cable and insert the plug into these holes:

O O

You may need to push them carefully free first, using a pencil. (You see, there is still a use for pencils!) Once connected, you will be able to use current thoughts to charge up your fantasy battery – just let your eyes close a while and let the pocket socket provide the mental energy you need. As we all know, Constant usage assaults your Battery. Everything costs in this world and even those who think they may enjoy limitless freedom need to be charged regularly. As the Light Brigade found out to their cost, even a torch needs more batteries than an artillery regiment. Just fifteen minutes charging will help you to turn this:

. . . .

. . . .

. .

. .

. . . .

. . . .

into this: Once upon a time there were three Bears, known to the Police as Daddy Bear, Mummy Bear and Babe Bear.

One day the three Bears came home to their cottage and found that a dumb blonde had broken in during their

absence and had totally ravaged the furnishings, leaving plates of half-eaten porridge all over the kitchen

and an unmade bed with soiled bedding. "Who the f*ck has been eating MY Porridge?" roared Daddy

Bear in a psychopathic rage. "Who the Hell has made such a mess of MY tidy Kitchen?" wailed Mummy

Bear, disconsolately picking up pieces of broken bowl and looking for a cloth with which to wipe up the

spilled and congealed and coagulated oatmeal porridge. Babe Bear said nothing; he had read a story like

this once a long time ago – or had it been read to him? - and he was already halfway up the stairs to see

if the Blonde was maybe still there in the bed....

So – Reading uses Energy, like any other activity, but with this Story with its inbuilt Socket you should be able to maintain power levels for much longer. Happy Reading!

MORAL:- Why? Fie!

****

No. 466 THE BUZZ

One of the irritating things which can happen to you, at any time but

zzzeeeeeeeeeeeeeeeeeeeeeeeeeeeeeeeeeeeeeeeeeeeeeeeeeeeeeeeeeeeeeeeeeeeeeeeeeeeeeeeeeeeeeeeeeeeeeeeee

especially as one gets older, is to hear a constant high

zzzeeeeeeeeeeeeeeeeeeeeeeeeeeeeeeeeeeeeeeeeeeeeeeeeeeeeeeeeeeeeeeeeeeeeeeeeeeeeeeeeeeeeeeeeeeeeeeeee

-pitched buzzing or droning noise in the background all the time. It

zzzeeeeeeeeeeeeeeeeeeeeeeeeeeeeeeeeeeeeeeeeeeeeeeeeeeeeeeeeeeeeeeeeeeeeeeeeeeeeeeeeeeeeeeeeeeeeeeeee

goes through your head constantly as though there is an angry insect

zzzeeeeeeeeeeeeeeeeeeeeeeeeeeeeeeeeeeeeeeeeeeeeeeeeeeeeeeeeeeeeeeeeeeeeeeeeeeeeeeeeeeeeeeeeeeeeeeeee

stuck in your ears or someone is sawing laboriously

zzzeeeeeeeeeeeeeeeeeeeeeeeeeeeeeeeeeeeeeeeeeeeeeeeeeeeeeeeeeeeeeeeeeeeeeeeeeeeeeeeeeeeeeeeeeeeeeeeee

through a large pane of glass just outside the window. It brings back

zzzeeeeeeeeeeeeeeeeeeeeeeeeeeeeeeeeeeeeeeeeeeeeeeeeeeeeeeeeeeeeeeeeeeeeeeeeeeeeeeeeeeeeeeeeeeeeeeeee

memories of those first times one had to sit in a dentist's chair as a

zzzeeeeeeeeeeeeeeeeeeeeeeeeeeeeeeeeeeeeeeeeeeeeeeeeeeeeeeeeeeeeeeeeeeeeeeeeeeeeeeeeeeeeeeeeeeeeeeeee

child and hear the tiny fast whirring drill starting up,

zzzeeeeeeeeeeeeeeeeeeeeeeeeeeeeeeeeeeeeeeeeeeeeeeeeeeeeeeeeeeeeeeeeeeeeeeeeeeeeeeeeeeeeeeeeeeeeeeeee

even before it came close to you or into you – the noise, not the

zzzeeeeeeeeeeeeeeeeeeeeeeeeeeeeeeeeeeeeeeeeeeeeeeeeeeeeeeeeeeeeeeeeeeeeeeeeeeeeeeeeeeeeeeeeeeeeeeeee

pain, was distressing enough. Or maybe it is like a kettle boiling in a

zzzeeeeeeeeeeeeeeeeeeeeeeeeeeeeeeeeeeeeeeeeeeeeeeeeeeeeeeeeeeeeeeeeeeeeeeeeeeeeeeeeeeeeeeeeeeeeeeeee

neighbour's flat – but he never goes to turn the bloody thing off!

zzzeeeeeeeeeeeeeeeeeeeeeeeeeeeeeeeeeeeeeeeeeeeeeeeeeeeeeeeeeeeeeeeeeeeeeeeeeeeeeeeeeeeeeeeeeeeeeeeee

Initially one wonders whether a refrigerator is maybe droning

zzzeeeeeeeeeeeeeeeeeeeeeeeeeeeeeeeeeeeeeeeeeeeeeeeeeeeeeeeeeeeeeeeeeeeeeeeeeeeeeeeeeeeeeeeeeeeeeeeee

electrically to itself.... one of those noises in the kitchen, in the

zzzeeeeeeeeeeeeeeeeeeeeeeeeeeeeeeeeeeeeeeeeeeeeeeeeeeeeeeeeeeeeeeeeeeeeeeeeeeeeeeeeeeeeeeeeeeeeeeeee

house that you simply take for granted and don't even consciously

zzzeeeeeeeeeeeeeeeeeeeeeeeeeeeeeeeeeeeeeeeeeeeeeeeeeeeeeeeeeeeeeeeeeeeeeeeeeeeeeeeeeeeeeeeeeeeeeeeee

realise it is there until perhaps the machine in question stops. We get

Zzzeeeeeeeeeeeeeeeeeeeeeeeeeeeeeeeeeeeeeeeeeeeeeeeeeeeeeeeeeeeeeeeeeeeeeeeeeeeeeeeeeeeeeeeeeeeeeeeee used to the distant hum of motor vehicles on a motorway

zzzccccccccccccccccccccccccccccccccccccccccccccccccccccccccccccccccccccccccccccccccccc

somewhere in the valley or to aeroplanes flying overhead, to the

zzzccccccccccccccccccccccccccccccccccccccccccccccccccccccccccccccccccccccccccccccccccc

extent that we barely notice them anymore – or indeed sometimes

zzzccccccccccccccccccccccccccccccccccccccccccccccccccccccccccccccccccccccccccccccccccc

realise with a shock that the background noise has suddenly ceased

zzzccccccccccccccccccccccccccccccccccccccccccccccccccccccccccccccccccccccccccccccccccc

leaving an almost uncomfortable silence – but with chronic tinnitus

zzzcccccccccccccccccccccccccccrccccccccccccccccccccccccccccccccccccccccccccccccccccccc

the low humming in the background remains a constant irritant. But

zzzccccccccccccccccccccccccccccccccccccccccccccccccccccccccccccccccccccccccccccccccccc

that's the way it is. From ear to ear and back again.

Zzzccccccccccccccccccccccccccccccccccccccccccccccccccccccccccccccccccccccccccccccccccc

MORAL:- Be grateful for the occasional refreshing Silence......

****

Weacleteeer Re Oetehe Seccheleled e e e e e e

No. 467   DATA RETENTION

Welcome to this **Story Portal.** This **Story Portal** enables you to access thousands of Online Stories which have been automatically Downloaded to your Eyes. Ensure the link to the Brain is connected (Ultra Sleepy Brain or USB) or use our App to ensure instant access to all the **Thousands** of Stories from Ey to Zee. Whether asleep or awake, the Stories from our **Story Portal** will flash before and behind your eyes simultaneously.

Our Stories include separate categories for Children's, Bedtime, Adventure, Western Adventure, Space Adventure, Science Fiction, Fantasy, Historical Romance, Modern Romance, Comic, Battles (Medieval), Battles (Historic), Battles (Modern) and Adult. You have unlimited access to all Stories at any time of Day or Night. With a simple click you can access whichever category you desire at this moment. Our Stories have been chosen by **Thousands** of Satisfied Customers who have enjoyed the Narratives, Plots and Endings and have recommended these to their **Thousands** of On-Line Friends. Please click Now to show 'Like' on our **Story Portal** Download Site.

LIKE.

This site employs Cookies to ensure that we can track you down wherever you are and hound you with unwanted advertising material, subliminally if necessary. We can now track you through your GPS settings. We also have access to all your banking information over the past six months, your credit rating, your credit card usage and all tickets purchased. Please click **HERE** to accept Terms and Conditions.

People who enjoyed this Story also enjoyed:

Art. 107/6/ba/6 Fish and Chips **!!!CLICK NOW TO ORDER!!!**

Art. 206/zz/54/1 Pint of Webster's Bitter **!!!CLICK NOW TO ORDER!!!**

Art. 338/4/201b Heinz Ketchup. 1-litre Bottle. **!!!CLICK NOW TO ORDER!!!**

Art. 226/9/cf/221 Sarsons Malt Vinegar 2-litre Bottle **!!!CLICK NOW TO ORDER!!!**

Art. 764/3/bah/34 Eyedrops. **!!!CLICK NOW TO ORDER!!!**

Art. 221/5/des/pu Soluble Headache Tablets. **!!!CLICK NOW TO ORDER!!!**

MORAL:- There are no Morals; This is Marketing!

****

LIKE!!!

No. 468 COLOURED BALLS

Time to start. Those two red balls in row six – click on them, they go. Good.

Now that brings the two blue balls that were above them down to be adjacent to the three blue balls in row seven. Click. Good. Gone.

You now have three yellow ones adjacent on rows five, six and seven. Click. Gone.

Now what? On row two there are two red balls near the top. Click. That brings the yellow one that was on top down to position six. Look! Row one, now row two, and then on row three there are two more – see that at the bottom of row three and on row four are two green ones? Click, that brings the yellow one down, good, click, all three gone. Good! Now row five moves left to become row four and all those to the right move with it.

You need to get those blue ones at the top right corner, row eight, down. Then there are two greens close on rows three and four. Get those down and it could bring you a total of six Reds all together, that gets more points.

Click that yellow one. The green drops down and the red after it. Then....

MORAL:- People spend HOURS playing with their balls like this. Why?

****

153

No. 469 A CONCEIT OF A RECEIPT

AESOP'S

STORY STORE

Fiction Dept.

Literature House,

Narrative Way.

Fri. 30.09.2017

Plot 1 x   10.00

Characters x 5 @ 12.50   62.50

Paragraphs x 11 @ 6.25   68.75

Nouns x 43@ 2.10   90.30

Adjectives x72 @ 1.80   129.60

Verbs x 33 @ 2.0   66.00

Punctuation Mxd Pack Med   25.00

* *

SUB TOTAL   452.15

Value Added Ability Tax   45.21

Author Authorisation   35.00

Spellcheck Services   38.00

Wordcount & Titling   42.57

* *

TOTAL TOTAL TOTAL   585.93

Thank you for Shopping at

AESOP'S

We look forward to serving you again.

For All Your Literary Needs!

****

See our Discounted Capital Letters!

Special Offer NOW ON.

MORAL:- There is a price for everything, even good literature.

****

No. 470   THE MULTIPLE CHOICE QUESTIONNAIRE

Tick only ONE Answer or Partial-Answer at a time.

Are you prepared to answer this Question? **[YES] [NO]**

Do you believe Multiple-Choice Questionnaires are a good way of assessing a student's knowledge? **[YES] [NO]**

Is it all basically a matter of Luck? **[YES] [NO]**

Could you just as well throw a Coin? **[YES] [NO]**

Do you think the answers are too simple? **[YES] [NO]**

Would you rather write out your own thoughts in your own words? **[YES] [NO]**

Is this an inane waste of time masquerading as academic testing? **[YES] [NO]**

Was it worth completing this Questionnaire? **[YES] [NO]**

Do you feel ticked off just ticking Boxes? **[YES] [NO]**

Have you ticked off your own Box? **[YES] [NO]**

MORAL:- You always have a choice in Life, though not always in Multiples. Yes? (or.... No?)

****

No. 471   NEWS!!!!!!!!!!!!!!!!!!

DAH-DAH-DEE-DEE-DEE-DA-DAH-DADADADA-DADA!

Hello-this-is-the-Some-o'clock-News-and-this-is-Ted-Blower-reading-it-in-a-staccato-fashion-at-great-speed-as-though-to-give-the-impression-that-you-need-to-hear-it-as-quickly-as-possible-in-case-it-stops-being-News!

And-here-is-the-News!!

This-morning-a-Politician-said-something-rude-and-insulting-about-another-Politician.   Politicians-are-reportedly-shocked-and-dismayed-at-this-state-of-affairs.   Here-is-an-interview-with-our-Parliamentary-Affairs-Correspondent-Harris-Commons.

"Thank you Ted. And today a major Politician said the following: [*Politician's voice in a slow drawl*] "It really is not very nice for a Politician to refer to another fellow Politician in such critical terms. This is not the correct mode of speech in such matters and someone should tell the two-faced slimy bastard that." I think that sums up the feeling of many Politicians very well. Back to you, Ted.''

Thank-you-Harris. Today-an-election-was-held-in-Someland-and-it-seems-as-though-one-Party-got-more-votes-than-the-other,-thus-giving-it-a-possible-majority-according-to-certain-analysts-who-took-a-poll-before-the-poll.-The-People's-Front-of-Remainia-is-seeking-autonomy-from-the-Brexit-Islands-although-political-commentators-state-that-this-would-only-be-realistic-with-the-construction-of-a-land-link-with-Belgium.

It-is-still-too-early-to-call-as-votes-are-still-being-counted-but-we-go-now-to-our-correspondent-at-the-vote.

"Thank-you-Ted-well-as-you-say-it-is-still-too-early-to-call-as-yet-since-the-votes-are-still-being-counted.-However-it-would-appear-that-one-side-has-certainly-gained-more-votes-than-the-other,-

although-we-cannot-yet-be-sure-which-one-or-indeed-how-many.-And-now-I-hand-you-back-to-the-studio."

Thank-you-and-I-am-sure-we-will-return-to-that-story-just-as-soon-as-there-is-something-to-report,-if-not-before.

Some-Economic-News.-A-Bank-reported-some-Figures-which-indicate-that-the-Economy-may-rise-or-fall-by-a-certain-per-cent.-The-DAX-and-the-Footsie-Index-moved-Up-and-Down-a-bit-during-the-day,-leading-to-speculation-that-they-might-go-Down-and-Up-a-bit-in-coming-days.

According-to-the-Dow-Jones-Index-this-may-continue-for-some-time-to-come,-leading-to-speculation-that-this-might-lead-to-speculation.

And-now-to-Sue-with-the-Weather.

"Thank you Ted, well, it seems that there will be Weather over the entire country. Later on this Weather may change in some places during the course of the day and it seems likely that by tomorrow or by the latest the day after the Weather may well have changed to some extent but for now we can safely say that we will stick with this Weather for the time being."

Thank-you-Sue. Now-some-urgent-Traffic-News. Police-say-that-many-roads-around-the-country-are-filled-with-Traffic-at-present-and-may-stay-so-for-some-time. They-are-currently-advising-drivers-to-stay-at-home-if-possible-if-they-wish-to-avoid-getting-stuck-in-heavy-traffic.-If you-have-to-drive-then-avoid-the-roads.

Now-to-Sport. Yesterday-a-lot-of-men-ran-around-a-field-for-an-hour-and-a-half-while-a-lot-of-spectators-watched-them. At-the-end-of-the-game-one-side-had-gained-more-points-than-the-other-and-was-declared-the-winner-and-may-rise-in-the-league-tables. As-one-of-the-captains-said: "It was a tough game but we won it and I am very pleased with the result."

And-that-is-all-we-have-time-for,   the-next-News-Bulletin-will-be-at-Something-Thirty. Good-Bye-and-don't-get-too-worried!

DAH-DAH-DEE-DEE-DEE-DA-DAH-DADADADA-DAD-DUMMMM!!!!!!!!!

MORAL:- Sometimes No News really <u>is</u> Good News.

****

No. 472   THE COPYIST

There was once a girl who spent her days standing in a tiny cubbyhole of an office at the end of a long carpet-tiled corridor making
photocopies photocopies photocopies photocopies photocopies
photocopies photocopies photocopies photocopies photocopies
photocopies photocopies photocopies photocopies photocopies
photocopies photocopies photocopies photocopies photocopies....

All through the working day people would come along from
different departments and thrust a bundle of papers at her, saying
"Can you copy this twenty times please?" "Can you copy this twenty
times please?" "Can you copy this twenty times please!" "Can you
copy this twenty times please" "Can you copy this twenty times
please" "Can you copy this twenty times please" "Can you copy this
twenty times please" "Can you copy this twenty times please" "Can
you copy this twenty time please" "Can you copy this twenty times
please" "Can you copy this twenty times please".... though
sometimes they forgot the "please" and then she would only do
nineteen or make the twentieth very faint.

"I'm tired of this," she thought to herself. "My life is so
repetititititive, always the same the same the same the same the
same the same... all day long long long long long long day after day
after day after day after day after day after day. Was there life before
A4? I seem to live on a staple diet and I do more binding than
bonding and even that is more of a spiral than a real coming
together." She took a pair of scissors and ripped open a packet of A4
Bond with especial vigour and not a little anger. It is hardly a
satisfying career, for a girl of even basic intelligence, to stand by a
grey plastic machine that goes Whumpf Whumpf Whumpf Whumpf
Whumpf Whumpf Whumpf Whumpf Whumpf Whumpf Whumpf
Whumpf Whumpf Whumpf Whumpf Whumpf Whumpf Whumpf
Whumpf Whumpf Whumpf Whumpf Whumpf Whumpf Whumpf
Whumpf Whumpf Whumpf Whumpf Whumpf Whumpf Whumpf
Whumpf Whumpf Whumpf Whumpf Whumpf Whumpf Whumpf
Whumpf Whumpf Whumpf all day spewing out one sheet sheet
sheet sheet sheet sheet sheet sheet sheet sheet sheet sheet sheet
sheet sheet sheet sheet sheet sheet sheet sheet sheet after another
after another after another after another after another after another

after another after another after another after another after another after another and then after her lunch break of forty-five minutes in the staff canteen on the fifth floor she had to go back to the little unventilated cubbyhole and stand there while it went Whumpf until five o'clock.... when she could gather up the copies, place them in a pile in a wire basket, place a label on top and turn the machine **OFFFFFFFF!!!**

She dreamed of a life with more creativity and originality, where there was more to choose between than just single-sided and double-sided. (She was of course still single-sided herself, partly because her boyfriend had turned out to be double-sided...). She could remove paper blockages, but her own life felt blocked. At home she had a hamster but no cats because that would make her think of copycats.... She went shopping but not to Copyshops. (Maybe coffeeshops - but even that was close...) She listened to the radio news but would not buy a newspaper because they came in copies. She dreamed of going on holiday to South America - to the Copycabana....

One day she snapped. "Change Cartridge" flashed the message. "That's JUST what I'll do," she said. And she inserted an empty ink cartridge, put a heavy coffee cup onto the 'Copy' button and walked out, leaving the machine to make thousands of copies that all looked like this:

Whumpf Whumpf Whumpf Whumpf Whumpf Whumpf Whumpf
Whumpf Whumpf Whumpf Whumpf Whumpf Whumpf Whumpf
Whumpf Whumpf Whumpf Whumpf Whumpf Whumpf Whumpf
Whumpf Whumpf Whumpf Whumpf Whumpf Whumpf Whumpf
Whumpf Whumpf Whumpf Whumpf Whumpf Whumpf Whumpf
Whumpf Whumpf Whumpf Whumpf Whumpf Whumpf Whumpf
Whumpf Whumpf Whumpf Whumpf Whumpf Whumpf Whumpf
Whumpf Whumpf Whumpf Whumpf Whumpf Whumpf Whumpf
Whumpf Whumpf Whumpf Whumpf Whumpf Whumpf Whumpf
Whumpf Whumpf Whumpf Whumpf Whumpf Whumpf Whumpf
Whumpf Whumpf Whumpf Whumpf Whumpf Whumpf Whumpf
Whumpf Whumpf Whumpf Whumpf Whumpf Whumpf Whumpf
Whumpf Whumpf Whumpf Whumpf Whumpf Whumpf Whumpf
Whumpf Whumpf Whumpf Whumpf Whumpf Whumpf Whumpf
Whumpf Whumpf Whumpf Whumpf Whumpf Whumpf Whumpf
Whumpf Whumpf Whumpf Whumpf Whumpf Whumpf Whumpf
Whumpf Whumpf Whumpf Whumpf Whumpf Whumpf Whumpf
Whumpf Whumpf Whumpf Whumpf Whumpf Whumpf Whumpf
Whumpf Whumpf Whumpf Whumpf Whumpf Whumpf Whumpf
Whumpf Whumpf Whumpf Whumpf Whumpf Whumpf Whumpf
Whumpf Whumpf Whumpf Whumpf Whumpf Whumpf Whumpf
Whumpf Whumpf Whumpf Whumpf Whumpf Whumpf Whumpf
Whumpf Whumpf Whumpf Whumpf Whumpf Whumpf Whumpf
Whumpf Whumpf Whumpf Whumpf Whumpf Whumpf Whumpf
Whumpf Whumpf Whumpf Whumpf Whumpf Whumpf Whumpf
Whumpf Whumpf Whumpf Whumpf Whumpf Whumpf Whumpf
Whumpf Whumpf Whumpf Whumpf Whumpf Whumpf Whumpf
Whumpf Whumpf Whumpf Whumpf Whumpf Whumpf Whumpf
Whumpf Whumpf Whumpf Whumpf Whumpf Whumpf Whumpf
Whumpf Whumpf Whumpf Whumpf Whumpf Whumpf Whumpf
Whumpf Whumpf Whumpf

till they filled up the room, then the corridor, then reached to the lift shaft, then filled this and eventually the entire office block was filled with blank photocopies until the floors began to collapse

under

the

weig

h

t

MORAL:- Sometimes you can copy but you can't cope.

****

At least some trees were hurt in the making of this copy. I hope you feel suitably guilty.

No. 473   THE POLICY

THE RELIABLE
INSURANCE

PARTNERSHIP

(Limited Liability Partnership)

(Registered in Cayman Islands)

Auto Protection Policy No. W0r7h1e55/5h1T

Your **RELIABLE** Insurance Policy

covers you against all risks and allows you to relax with peace of mind! Enjoy the Freedom of the Road, secure in the knowledge that any Unexpected Incidents will not lead to further distress or loss. You and your loved ones will enjoy the comfort that comes from knowing that you have taken the right precautions against all dangers and shocks.

You are advised to **keep this Policy Document somewhere safe** where you know you will not be able to find it if needed.

Your **RELIABLE** Insurance Policy

Exclusions:

All damage caused by Accidents; all damage caused by Vandalism or deliberately by Self or Third Parties; All damage to the Inside or the Outside of the car; All damage caused to the Motor or Suspension. All damage caused by or to Third Parties. All damage due to Natural Causes. All damage caused by War, Terrorism, Fire, Flood, Earthquake, Tremors caused by Nuclear Tests, Radiation, Sunlight, Frost, Fog, Tides, Tsunami, Wind, Lightning, Meteors, Insects, Animals, Reptiles, Birds, Excessive Temperature, Excessive Dryness, Pedestrians, Cyclists, Motorists, Haulage Contractors, Construction Machines, Alien Invaders or their Spacecraft. Excessive Excess. All damage caused by Worms, Beetles, Centipedes, Woodlice, Woodworm, Moths or Moles. Damage caused by Rust or Corrosion or Perishing of Rubber and Seals or Wearing; Damage caused by Oil Spill or Fuel Spill. Damage caused by Use of Incorrect Fuel or Lubricants; Damage caused by poor Maintenance or Repair, whether by Self or in a Workshop; Damage caused by fitting of spare parts, whether authorised or unauthorised; Damage caused by Children and Infants, by the Sick and Infirm and by Pets or other Creatures as defined by the Biological Life Forms Act 1929 §128.4-8. Damage due to poor Street Lighting, poor Road Surface, Repairs being undertaken to Roads, Bridges, Gates, Toll Gates, Level Crossing and other Barriers, Fencing, Tunnels, Bollards (Permanent or Temporary), Drainage Covers, Gutters, Utilities, raised Road Markings, or Pavements. Damage caused by distractions due to Map Reading or GPS systems. Damage caused by Distraction due to listening to Radio or Music (CD or Cassette) while driving. Damage caused in Car Parks whether Public or Private. Damage caused by Birds or Insects on Windscreen. Damage caused in Car Washes and Workshops. Damage caused while Car is on Lorry or Railway Wagon for Transport. Any damage caused by Roof Racks or Cycle Racks. Damage to Aerials. Loss of Small Items behind Seat Cushions.

Your **RELIABLE** Insurance Policy

Health Exclusions. All conditions (including Eye Strain) caused by or exacerbated by Reading Insurance Policies. Any injuries caused by Accidents while In, On or Under the Vehicle; while Driving or as Passenger or while Loading or Unloading the Vehicle. Any Headaches caused by bright Sunlight; any Stiffness caused by Draughts. All damage or loss caused by Forgetfulness, Stress, Fatigue, Sexual Fantasies and other Daydreaming, Sneezing, Insect Stings or Irritating Buzzing, Poor Weather, Pregnancy, Infertility, Distraction, Lack of Sleep, Other Drivers, Pedestrians, Cyclists (whether Unicycle, Bicycle or Tricycle), Moped Drivers, Roller-Skaters and Skateboarders, Pets or other Road Users. Attempts to become Pregnant while Driving are also excluded.

The Policy Holder will be liable for all Administrative Costs connected with the processing of any Claim and any Costs incurred by the Company in checking Information and Claims, gathering Repair Estimates, Bank Charges and Currency Exchange Costs, plus Investigator Costs including Professional Fees, Travel, Postage, Telephones, Telefax, Telex, Printing and/or Photocopying (2D or 3D) and Miscellaneous Charges as Defined under Para. 45/b(ii) of the General Rules and Conditions.

Your **RELIABLE** Insurance Policy

is not **protected by Bond**. The **RELIABLE** **Insurance Company** is not **covered by the Insurance Companies** (Avoidance of Swindling) Acts of 1951, 1963, 1990, 2012 § 184-203. The **RELIABLE** **Insurance Company** is not **registered at Companies House in accordance with Board of Trade regulations** 1932, 1935, 1967.

Your **RELIABLE** Insurance Policy

The Company is <u>R</u>eliable, which means it is not itself Liable but transfers all responsibility to the Policy Holder.

Thank you for choosing to purchase

Your **RELIABLE** Insurance Policy!

No. 474   ALLERGIES

There was once a man who discovered that he was allergic to the 'Letter-between-e-and-g'. Not only that, but even though he could cope with the letters 'between-o-and-q', and 'between-g-and-i', in moderation, should they be placed together then the sound had almost the same result, so that he came out in spots and pustules and his head would begin to swell. Many an author has a swollen head, but this was something not-the-same.

Now, Allegories are often praised as literary creations and Elegies are moving and often collected and later published, but a Letter-Allergy is not something to be sneezed at, even though one may do so on those occasions when it arises. One is compelled to employ longer and more complex sentences in order to convey a meaning that would be much simpler were one to be able to employ a simple short part-of-a-sentence or particular letters that instead need to be avoided. There are even additional complications - as an example, what is one to do with the combination with 'g' and 'h' when they appear together in the word that begins 'enou' and means 'adequate' but SOUNDS like the letter we mean?

This letter comes quite, er, many times in the English language and it is hard to avoid it totally. As any dictionary will show you, many words begin with it. Others end with it, even doubled – as an example, the man wanted to inhale through his nose the powder known as snu** but could not even ask at a Chemist's whether they stocked this material. Most irritating was that when he wanted to express his anger at an event or occasion or something that had happened to him, he could only say "Ucking hell!" and this made people lau.... er... react in an amused manner.

He had to have special keyboards made at great expense so that there was no risk whereby his, er, digit or even just its tip might come into contact with a key with the letter in question. This is expensive but necessary should one wish to be able to type at all. One needs to look at packets to ensure that they do not bear the label

'Caution! Could contain Certain Letters!'; There is loneliness and social isolation to endure: One has companions and colleagues but no 'riends'. It might be just about bearable with a 'z' but the letter in question is used in words to indicate choice and uncertainty, or a place where one has departed, or a matter one has provided to another person or purpose - very common words indeed in any normal narrative or conversation. Even a direction, the opposite to 'right'. I hope I do not have to be too detailed here. Ironically, I cannot just spell it out, because this is the whole issue. But how can one enter a conversation with another person when one is never sure whether this 'letter-between-e-and-g may not be spoken inadvertently by the other? And the moment it is uttered it could lead to the bodily reactions outlined above - one is constantly in a state... er... in a condition laden with concern and worry. Despite taking great care to avoid this letter it is sometimes difficult - oh heck - Aaaargh! Doubled!! My head! My head!

MORAL:- Allergies do not respect Morals.

****

No. 475 UP IN THE CLOUDS

Good evening and welcome to this Story. My name is Walter Rothschild and I shall be your Author on this Story in this PTN Print-Text Narrative Mark 1a Book. Helping you with the text will be the Publisher and the Proof-Reader and if you have any problems, please just turn to them, they will be pleased to deal with any queries you might have. We welcome especially any Frequent Reader Card-Holders who have borrowed this book from their Library with their cards.

On your dust jacket you will find brief details of the Author and some comments from favourable critics, please read these carefully before opening the Book as these will help you appreciate the skills involved. Should you get a little bored the Contents page will lead you to the next Chapter Headings; look now for where your nearest Chapter Heading is, as it may be already behind you. Should it be necessary, then read this Story yourself first before reading it to your children.

We are due to start this Story in about ten minutes, local time; until then please relax. We expect this Story to last about Ten Minutes and hope to reach the end punctually. There are some exciting bits so please keep your seat belts on when you get to those paragraphs! In addition, some of the characters have turbulent pasts so you are advised to take care. Emotional baggage may shift or become exposed during the course of the narrative. A word about Refreshments - Our special 'Coffee and Biscuits' will be served when you make them before sitting down to read.

Today we shall start with some introductions, then turn backwards a bit to recapitulate some previous events before heading onwards and rising towards the Climax, following which we shall start the descent to reality. We are not expecting any plot twists beyond the ordinary. Those of you with Sequels to read, please contact your local bookstore or online provider to gain access.

We have just heard from Page Control that we can start at Once Upon a Time. Well, that's it from the Write Desk so, sit back and enjoy your read! Thank you for choosing to read with us today.

'' 'Once upon a Time………………

.************************

No. 476   THE BIO-FOIBLE   **C**

Your **BIO**-Foible. This Story is a <u>**Free Range**</u> Story - unlike many Narratives which are from their very beginnings bound by conventions, in this tale the Ideas may range freely. No artificial Additives, Colourings or Preservatives have been used. It is classed as 'Bio' which means it was once a lively story before it was placed humanely onto this two-dimensional recycled paper using non-metallic inks and it includes living characters. The story contains no additional sweetness or coyness. It is guaranteed free of all authenticides. Only authorised Authors have been used. Vegetarians and Vegans may read this Story without problems, as may those on Low-Salt, Low-Fat, Low-Sugar, Low-Calorie, Low-Life, Low-Interest and Low-Intelligence literary diets. The plot may be digested without difficulties. Only simple Metaphors have been employed and the Spelling has been carefully checked for any potential nonconformities.

Our Stories are all hand-written in natural daylight, using mainly original ideas, locally-sourced. Any ideas that may have been acquired from other sources have been done so in accordance with Fair Read principles to aid indigenous authors. The basic plots have all been recycled, several times.

The **C** Symbol indicates that this is classed as a Childlike or Childish Story, authenticated and guaranteed by the Society of Children's Authors. This Story contains no Death, Violence, Blood or Gore and all Characters remain alive at the end. It may be given to Children over the age of 4 and sensitive Adults with a mental age from 10 upwards. No Proof-Readers or Type-Setters have been hurt in the making of this Story.

Large Print Versions are Available on Request. For Braille and Audio Versions please apply to the Publisher.

MORAL:- It is one form of middle-class intellectual self-righteous high morality to enjoy only Bio-Fiction as well as Biography. The Feelgood Factor and Political Correctness always take priority over literary merit and for such people the Bioble is more authoritative than the Bible.

****

No. 477 UNVITAL STATISTICS

Statistics is the study of Numbers on the basis that Numbers are more important than anything else and that Everything, but Everything can be reduced to numbers, to figures, digits and proportions. Statisticians are people who believe in Numbers; They pick their homes on the basis of the statistics for potential break-ins or the average rise in prices or rents over the past five years; They pick their girlfriends and partners on the basis of their so-called 'vital statistics' which in fact not only fail utterly to describe their characters, sense of humour, ambitions, creativity or even fertility, but also say nothing at all about their *vita*, their lives, since they describe only the measurements around their bosoms, their hips and what is politely referred to as the 'taille' for all those taille-end Charlies (or 'bummers' in more colloquial terms). After all, most statisticians when referring to "the bottom line" will assume it is horizontal, whereas any connoisseur of the human body knows it is vertical.

Statisticians are, in fact, statistically considered, rather sad people.

Statistics demonstrate that the chances of your having read this far are 59.4% if you are aged 12-20, 69.5 % if you are aged 21 - 50 and 92.4% if you are aged 60 or over and have nothing better to do.

Statisticians devote their lives to collecting data rather than experiences. They note down levels or rates and percentages as though these are the most important things in life. They exchange data with each other or challenge each other's statistical findings and rather anal analyses because they have nothing else to talk about. It goes almost without saying that they base their religious life and theology mainly upon the Book of Numbers. And yet a concern with statistics is essentially static.

Statistics demonstrate that if you are aged 12-20 you have a 37.3% chance of having read this far, if aged 21-50 a 48.1% and, if you are over 60 and still have nothing better to do, then 81.7%. Statistically you are also 28.32% likely to have re-read the first paragraph to see if you have really understood it the first time and there is a 29.6% chance that you would really rather have a good cup of tea at this point.

Statisticians often use old-fashioned technology such as chalk on blackboards to make their points, though 63.2% also use whiteboards with coloured markers. They prefer ordinary graph papers to pornography papers. Their concern is with quantity and never with quality - even when discussing the quality of something they do so on the basis of the quantity of responses indicating that consumers found the quality good / acceptable / fair / poor. They know the variations in the prices of artworks but not the meaning of art. They can measure the statistics of life expectation but not the expectations that people have of their lives. They measure length, not depth.

Statistics demonstrate that if you are aged 12-20 you will not have read this far at all; if aged 21-50 then 23.6 % will have read to this point. It is only the over-60s of whom one can say that 74.1 % are likely to have spent the past eight minutes reading the whole of this text, for such people have time to spend and not to waste. Or is it the other way around? I had better check the statistics.

MORAL:- Statistics are generally considered better than Lies or Damned Lies because they look so much more impressive! People are 97.3% more likely to be taken in by a falsified statistic than by a downright lie. At least, 63.8% of them admit so.

****

No. 478   A LITERARY TABOO

One of the things which Authors hate to talk about is that of Fictional Dysfunction - also known as Narrative Style Dysfunction. Very few Authors are prepared to open up and speak about this experience, which is usually considered to be embarrassing and not something to share with others - yet it is much more common than is normally assumed.

One author describes it as follows: "You get an idea in your mind, but before you can get it stiffened and shaped and keep it there so that you can get it down on paper, it just sort of goes flabby. It's like trying to write a murder story without enough blood in it." Others say "You get started all right with an opening paragraph or two, and then either you cannot get the story up to speed, or you just can't keep it up until the end."

It is no wonder that those whose livelihoods depend upon producing a steady stream of words onto paper find this more than just a minor embarrassment. Several techniques have been proposed by specialists to overcome this 'block', apart from writing in block letters, but they do have their down sides as well as their up ones. For example, composing sexual fantasies may assist a writer to continue a Romantic narrative, but these should not be used in books for Children - and <u>especially</u> not if the fantasies involve children! This is where one needs a good and discreet editor and proof-reader. Likewise fantasies of murder and mayhem may get the creative juices flowing but one does not want to stimulate a real murder, unless perhaps it may be of the neighbour whose noise is distracting one from writing.

A story which dribbles to a standstill part-way through is unsatisfying both to the author and the reader - not to mention the publisher. The Reader (who is, after all, the one who invests money to purchase the completed work) especially is usually looking forward to at least one good climax per volume, or in some cases (involving volumes of short stories) several climaxes one after the other. When the narrative just dwindles to a self-conscious description of picturesque landscapes or inner depressive moods with an overabundance of similes but no real action, when the text becomes more adjectival or even adverbial than truly verbal, when the action is verbose and punctuated only by punctuation, then disappointment sets in and in the longer term this can also affect sales of any sequels and lead to a loss of contract and self-confidence. The relationship between an Author and a Publisher can be a fragile one if, as one might put it, one of them "cannot deliver the goods" on time when desired, even through no fault of their own.

An Author who is under stress, working fast towards a deadline, may find that his writing becomes mechanical but not truly creative, he is cutting corners and rushing; An author who is getting elderly and suffering occasional memory loss may forget which character did what in a previous volume or even chapter; Those who are on a later volume of a lengthy series may find that the repetitiveness leads to a loss of originality and excitement - one of the issues is that this can hit any Author, even ones who have had long and successful and productive careers to date. Distractions of any sort will of course have an effect on textual performance and reduce productivity..... As one put it, "You can always add a full stop - but can you start the next sentence? It's a new challenge each and every time."

All that we can recommend is that Authors who face this problem should also face up to it, open up about it and share their fears and problems with others. They will soon find that it is more common than they think, that many a novelist has retreated to short stories because the length of a full novel has grown too intimidating, that many a Publisher or Agent has had to encourage, persuade, support, cajole and sometimes just cuddle an Author to get them to the state where they can relax, let the destructive stresses wash away and the creativity re-emerge from wherever it has gone. And sometimes one just needs to make a pause and wait for things to return to how they had used to be.

MORAL:- Sorry, I really can't think of one right now.....oh, it's so frustrating......

****

No. 479 THE DO'S AND DOTS OF COMMUNICATION

Samuel Morse was a painter (*this is true*) and a dashing young inventor. Together with his wife Dorothy, whom he called Dot, he was working on a new idea for the use of the new-fangled electric telegraph machine. He had thought of an ingenious system whereby each Letter could be represented by a number of Dots, related to their place in the alphabet - thus . for **A**, .. for **B**, ... for **C**, ... for **D** and so forth. Unfortunately, this system was imperfect; firstly, it made no allowance for CAPITAL or small letters, it made the provision of digits for Numbers impossible, and by the time you got to, say, the letter **M**, represented by .... it was frankly unwieldy and one was running out of fingers. And that was only halfway through! And what about ümläüts, çedillas, grâves and other àccénts? It could drive a man wild.

It was a tricky problem and he thought long and hard about it while they went one evening to a performance of the new opera 'Turandot' at the opera house. (*This was quite an achievement in itself, since it wasn't performed until 1926; But scientists and those concerned with invisible forms of electronic communication through cables or the ether have their ways and means that we other mortals cannot comprehend.*) The plot was complicated and so during the first interval Dot read to him from the programme booklet the summary printed there and, finishing, closed the booklet with the words "Well, that seems to be the long and the short of it."

A brainwave struck him and, as any internet user of modern times will tell you, you have to be a good surfer when a real brainwave comes along. "I must dash!" he said to Dot and left the opera house on the dot of 9.30p-dot-m-dot. He had had a bit of a code id de dose developing in any case and his work had been a bit slapdash of late though, as a painter, he had fallen for the new pointillistic system of a lot of painted dots on the canvas, the hairy predecessor of the modern electronic pixel system. He went to his desk and looked at a blank piece of paper. "Oh, dash it!" he thought to himself and picked up a pencil........ (Note: These dots represent just the passing of time and are not to be read otherwise.) Then he drew a line - and then another --. One was, as he measured it, shorter than the other, but as if to compensate, the other was longer than the first. This was an interesting new principle. Bending over the table he set to work, tapping the floor with his toes as he did so to a new rhythm that would change the world.

Next morning when Dot came to breakfast he said, "-. --- --- -.. -- --- .-. -. .. -. --. !" *

To his surprise, and perhaps also his dismay, she looked him in the eyes, thought for a moment, and then responded: ".-- .... .- - .- .-. . .-. - --- ..- - .-. -.-- .. -. -. - --- ... .- -.--?" **

Samuel was rather taken aback and asked ".... --- .-- -.. .. -.. -.-- --- ..- -.- -. --- .--?" ***

She smiled gently and answered ".-- --- — . -. -.-. .- -. .- .-.. .-- .- -.-- ... .-. . .-- -.. - ... .-. .... ..- ... -... .- -. -.. ... !" ****

To which he had no answer at all.

The first experiment to try out this system outdoors was not very successful because, having built a transmitter out of some odd pieces of brass and left-over picture frame, he discovered messages could not be effectively transmitted until there was a receiver at the other end as well. (*The first telephone suffered from the same problem, as Guglielmo Marconi found out to his frustration; plus, you could not get a crossed line until you had at least four apparatuses.*) He thought he had had it tapped but this was incorrect. (*Incidentally, tapping telephone conversations is not the same as tapping morse telegraph messages; One is a sort of hot tap, the other a cold tap and they do not mix. It's something to do with the plug.*) For a while he felt more morose than morse as he inspected the problem - the first morse inspector if not inspector morse - but eventually with the addition of some more cables and some solid soldering the issue was resolved and by the end of the first week of experimentation the operator was already up to a rate of words per minute rather than minutes per word.

The rest is, well, history, for almost no-one uses it any more. Progress is remorseless and in an age of antisocial social media all are more or less morseless. This all part of the rich (or formerly-rich) Tappestry of life. But for a while railway telegraphers and ships were busily bipping and beeping at each other, and generals would call for their telegraphists on the battlefields, "A morse! A morse! My kingdom for a morse!" Samuel himself grew rich, though he was soon in his dotage and she too was a bit dotty by the end.

MORAL:- Sorry, must dash. I'll send you a tweet later... **-... -.-- .** !

....

(*Key*:-

* Good Morning!

** What are you trying to say?

*** How did you know?

**** Women can always read their husbands!)

****

No. 480   SPONSORSHIP

Welcome to our 2018 Personalised Story Series. We are currently seeking Sponsors for these Tales.

Have you ever wished to have a Story featuring You and your Loved Ones? Now is your chance. You have a choice of Glass, Silver, Gold and Platinum Sponsorship. Consider the following Options:

Glass.

For only €100 as a **Glass** Sponsor you and your political opinions can appear in the Story. For example:

"It was a dark and stormy night. Mr. [Terence Bowler] and his wife [Florence] looked out of the window. What mischief could be abroad on a night like this? After all, for any true Brexit supporter, ALL matters connected with 'abroad' are full of the most evil mischief....."

Silver.

For **Silver** (€250) you can be the Hero of the Story.

"[Mr. Terence Bowler] blew the smoke from the end of his revolver and looked keenly into the distance. "Oh, [Terence]!" gasped [Florence], staring at him adoringly. "You are my hero! You have saved me! I will go with you, wherever you want!" Bending low he scooped her off her feet and placed her over his left shoulder. "That's just what I wanted to hear," he said......."

Gold. (€500)

For **Gold** you can also make the Villain a person of your choice. This is the chance to get back at any unpleasant Boss, clinging Relative, annoying Neighbour, etc.

"[Terence Bowler] sat back in his chair at the breakfast table, opened the newspaper and scanned the front page. "I see that old bugger [Matt Painter] has got himself murdered," he said with some satisfaction. "The old bugger had it coming to him, no-one at the firm liked him. I wonder which one of them did it? Maybe it was a joint effort."

"Oh, and his horrible wife too," said [Florence Bowler]. "The one with the eyes too close together. And always so proud of having come from the aristocracy of Sri Lanka! I'm sure she deserves this, the bitch. She was so rude to me at the last Staff Christmas Party!"

He scanned the news item. It seemed to have been a particularly gruesome and brutal double murder. [Terence] read some excerpts to [Florence] as they both enjoyed a second cup of coffee. "The head was found......."

Platinum.

As a **Platinum** Sponsor (€1,000) you are able also to purchase the Title of the Story, thus:

[TERENCE BOWLER] AND THE MISSING CORPSE.

"Detective Chief Inspector [Terence Bowler] looked keenly at the floor of the Library. Around him stood Lady Darnley and her butler, Jenkins, the housemaid Muriel Smithson and the Cook, Mrs. Badgett. He turned to his assistant [Florence]. "So," he murmured, almost to himself. "This is the spot where Lord Darnley was found, expired, at 5.30 this morning? But where is he now? Lord Darnley was certainly no Nobody and so for him now to have become a No Body is strange, most strange. What do you make of this, eh, [Florence]?"

"Well Sir," replied Detective Constable [Florence Bowler], "We know that the body showed no signs of violent struggle, according to Achmet Patel Petersen the Footman – where is he now, I wonder? Indeed, Petersen told me" – she consulted her official notebook – "that he suspected poisoning. The expression on Lord Darnley's face, he said, and the fact that the remains of one of Mrs. Badgett's tongue-and-pickle sandwiches was still on a plate on the table, led to this presumption on his part. The pickle, of course, could well have been employed to disguise any flavours of poison."

"Well thought through, [Florence]," said [Mr. Terence Bowler] with a touch of admiration. "We'll make a good detective out of you yet! Now,...."

You may also choose to sponsor just a *Sentence* or an individual *Paragraph*. In such cases the result may look like this:

"[Terence Bowler]!" he called across the crowded room. "Yes, that's me," replied [Terence Bowler] "As I live and breathe, what has [Terence Bowler] been doing since we last met? "Well," said [Terence Bowler], "after university I set up my own firm, [Terence Bowler Holdings] and am glad to say that things are going well......."

Or:

"Many men have worked hard for their success," said the Minister. "And their loyalty to the party and their love for their country is beyond doubt. I speak to you today about [Terence Bowler] to whom I am happy and proud to present this Order today. Rarely has an award been better deserved. [Terence Bowler] is a shining example of the type of man whose merits are beyond question and who has been overlooked for too long. So, [Terence Bowler], I congratulate you and your lovely wife [Florence] on this presentation." She turned to the man standing at her side at the podium, a man famous for his modesty and generosity to good causes, and smiled a wide Jamaican smile. "Would you care to say a few words yourself on this auspicious occasion?...."

Please Note: For reasons of literary legislation we are compelled to ensure Equality of Genders and Ethnic Background of characters (work on Third-Gender Issues will commence with the 2019 Series.)

Warning: Erotic incidents may only be incorporated into Stories intended for Adults Only. Explicit Sexual Fantasies and Acts of

Sexual Perversion are only available for Platinum-Plus Sponsors (€5,000). Illustrations to be negotiated separately.

For all Sponsorship questions please contact us on:
Sponsorship@Story4U.com

MORAL:- When it comes to being willing to sell your Creativity for Sponsored Lucre, it is clear that the word 'Moral' has no place.

****

No. 481   NO ENTRY

Welcome to **STORYPAGE.** By entering **STORYPAGE** you can access almost all of world Literature with a single Mouseclick!!

NOTICE: We use Cookies. By reading this far you have already accepted our Terms and Conditions. **Click on ACCEPT** even if you have not been bothered to try to read them. **WE GUARANTEE** to pass your personal details and reading habits to any commercial income source that we can find. **YOUR DATA IS** not **SAFE!**

To Enter this Story, enter **PASSWORD**:_____

Sorry this **PASSWORD** is Incorrect. Try again:_____

Have you forgotten your **PASSWORD**? Are you really that incompetent? Click **Here** and we can send you a new one:_____

You have only one more Attempt. Enter **PASSWORD** here:_____

Password Incorrect. Your Access has been denied. See your Story Provider for more details.

MORAL:- What a difference a single Word can make! A kind word, or even the wrong kind of word.

****

No. 482   A LOAD OF BULL

There was once a Bull who felt he was not like other Bulls. He was in a strange mooed. He knew what was expected of him by the farmer, but his heart was just not in it and sometimes this meant that the rest of him was not in it either. How can I explain it? He simply was not attracted to big udders. He did not get excited by cowslips or any other form of bovine lingerie. The atmosphere of milking sheds disgusted him and yet at the same time fascinated him. He had no desire to spend his days picking up Daisies or any other daft cow with a silly name. He yearned to be a Nobull savage. He was depressed, suffering from what Bovine Psychowlogists call an "Inabbullity to get horny at the right time."

Although cattle have been domesticated since ancient times, many of the old skills have been forgotten and few people specialise in this aspect of veteran veterinary science. It is known that calf love is strictly taboo and the herd instinct is to isolate and pillory any bull who shows interest in young and immature females. But there is much more to bovine sexuality than a load of bullocks and sometimes you just want to go with the buffalo. This is real and not just hyperbulle.

One day, suffering from a bout of post-cowtal depression, he approached a young bullock. "Could I interest you in some grass?" he said, moovingly. "I think I want to come out of the stall. There must be new fields for me. The one we have here is full of bullshit and no-one seems to care."

He felt strange inner stirrings. Licking his nose (his OWN nose I hasten to add), or at least the ring at the end of it, he wanted to grab the young bull by the horns. The youngster felt uneasy and ambullavent. He didn't want to be bullied. He was just at the stage where he was exploring his own identity. (This is a complex issue. For example: Bulls have an ambivalent attitude to Religion - many cows would secretly like to be Hindu, enjoying the privileges that come with being considered holy; Whereas bulls know only too well how often they have suffered and been sacrificed on the altars of

185

unaltarable traditions in the past. Similarly bulls and cows are vegetarians and know that they have a personal steak in this custom spreading. Essentially pacifist, they would prefer to avoid a bull fight; There are few cowpatriots and many trace their pedigrees to offshore interests in the Channel Islands, especially Jersey and Guernsey. But it's hard to hide when you are a bull.)

"Life's tough when you get older," he told the young fellow who was chewing his breakfast cud, again. "The farmer sends you out to cover the cows and he makes a cover charge for it but, between you and me and between the covers, it's not very romantic, it's a very seedy business, Two Pints Please, no romance at all."

"Not at all?" The young bullock sounded disappointed.

"God help us, they stuff the cows with hormones - who can find a fat cow attractive? They call it Bullimia but it's more 'Seen and Herd'. Not even proper privacy.

Sometimes all you see of your partner is her rump and I have to tell you, Hind sight is NOT one hundred per cent, whatever they tell you in those cock-and-bull stories at school. Trust me, I've been there, they expect you to feel bullish all the time, whatever your interest rate might be. In out, in out, wave it all about. Maybe the Jews are right to keep Meat and Milk separate. I would advise you to make some male friendships, find a proper relationship. It's not all balls, you know. Interested?"

Pretty soon he was biting the bull-ett and frisking around, enjoying life. His partner was still young and a bit green, but he showed a willing interest to learn. He had not yet understood that sooner or later Life can make mincemeat of us all.

I will end the narrative here as I don't want to put you off your cheeseburger or give you an embullism.

MORAL:- You will never read "Ann of Green Gay Bulls" the same way again.

****

No. 483   THE DREAM

There was once a Dream, or was there? I think there was, but it is
hard to be sure, it is difficult to remember, I am pretty sure there was
a Dream, there, once, but it is all so vague now, it is like it is
swimming away from me - swimming! Yes, I was swimming, in a
desert, on top of a mountain, and eating an ice cream while looking
out at the jungle. I think. Or was I at the Zoo? Somewhere, and
somehow I know I felt that I was there, but Where? And why was
Elvis Presley sitting across from me? Or was it Winston Churchill?
Whoever it was smiled at me and said - what was it they said? Do
you know, I KNOW it happened and at the time I felt absolutely
normal about it but now that I come to think of it.... There was a bit
when I was in a train, yes, looking out of the window, at the sea, but
we were underwater and a shark came towards me, or was it an
airship? If I close my eyes I can still almost see it now - almost -
almost - no, no, it's gone, but it WAS there, I'm sure, how is it I can
know that but I can't remember exactly what it was? But it was. Or
maybe it was the other one, when this woman with dark red hair was
smiling at me, and I felt so warm inside. Her name was.... was.... I
know I knew her name. It was.... no, I can't remember any more, but
we talked and she knew me and I knew her.... and then, when she
turned into my teacher from the third form I remembered her name
again, it was, it was..... well, never mind, it all came flooding back
in its way, but then we were in a rowing boat, first I was rowing,
then she was rowing, and the sun was shining until a storm came
and I was glad to come inside the porch out of the rain and I could
dry out in front of the log fire but first I had to move this massive
dog that was in front of the fire but then it was a bear and it turned
on me and then – or no, wasn't it before? Maybe it was – or maybe it
wasn't, or it... well, somehow I was standing on the balcony looking
out over the lake and watching an aeroplane landing on the
mountain and then these three chaps got out, one of them was
carrying a spear and another had a tray with a bottle and some
glasses on it and the third was carrying a chair, was it a canvas chair,
I think so, a folding one, and they all began singing, and I leaned
over the balcony, to listen better, and then a big spider was coming
towards me, and I was in shock and couldn't move! And I wanted to

scream but I couldn't, it felt like the floor was moving beneath me and I would fall down into a pit of spiders and snakes! And then ….

Then I was on the floor beside the bed with the duvet half on top of me.

MORAL:- We all need a Dream. We all have Dreams. But - Sometimes it is better to forget them quickly. God help you if your dreams ever become true! Wake up!

****

No. 484   MEMOIRS OF AN AMNESIAC

I was born in, er..... well, let me think, it was, no, no, it was, it must have been, let's count backwards a bit, I know it was before the er...

Well, the town was, yes, it was, well, big, don't you know, in a, er, in a smallish sort of way, yes, that's it, not too big, not too small, and I know I'll remember the name any moment now, it began with a 'P', I'm pretty sure, or was there a P in the middle? It's grown a bit now, of course, but in my day, when I was a child growing up there, it was, er, it had a sort of, well, you know, people liked being there because it was so, well, and there was a lot of industry, I believe, so jobs, making, er, was it hats? Or ships? Or blankets?

Anyway, I went to school, I think, can't remember much of that part of my life, it's all a bit of a blur frankly, a long time ago now, but I must have done all right because afterwards I went to the College, whatever it was called, and studied something-or-other for a while, I suppose, after all, I did get a degree at the end, I have the certificate somewhere, I know I put it somewhere, somewhere safe, haven't seen it for years though.

Now, when did I meet my wife? Come to think of it, where was that? I know I must have met her, because we got married in, in, whenever, and then we had three children. Or was it four? I can never remember their names. Anyway, a charming wife, very pleasant, a wonderful wife, I think, and she must have been a good mother too because the children, the children, yes, er, well, they all grew up somehow and went off. One is a teacher now, in, somewhere down south I think. Then my daughter, she got married I think, lives somewhere, begins with an 'M', Marsden? Manchester? Oh yes, Huddersfield, I knew I'd remember it.

People are kind, very kind, they say I did something very important with my life. Well, I am happy that they are so happy and interested,

189

I get a lot of questions from people, about the old times, when I was a, a, let me see now, what was it I did?

You know, it all seems so long ago now. I went to the Clinic the other day, I remember I had to fill in a form, one of the questions was 'Do you suffer from Amnesia?' Strange, I remember thinking about that, wondering whether I should tick the box or not. I mean, if I did, that would prove that I am all right really, yes? What? Did I tick the box? You know, I can't recall.

I am sure I have lived a very interesting life. I just wish I could remember some of it now and then.

MORAL:- Do you know, I cannot remember when my Amnesia was as bad as it is today?

****

No. 485   THE DIVERSE BEARS

Once upon a time there were Nine Bears. This was necessary for reasons of Diversity, in order to reflect all aspects of modern Society. There was Daddy Bear, Mummy Bear, Baby Bear, Mummy Bear's lover (and Baby's biological father), Daddy Bear's gay partner, Baby Bear's bisexual Cousin, Mother Bear's non-Binary Sister, Polar Bear who was a different colour to the others who were brown, being albino, and someone who being Transgender can only be called Bore because s/h/it kept talking about it, on and on and on. It was hard to bear any of them sometimes. Especially all crowded unbearably into a fairly small house.

Polar Bear likes white coffee and white sugar, whereas the other Bears prefer brown coffee and cane brown sugar. His friend Bi-Polar Bear who comes to visit sometimes takes both white and brown sugar and is in consequence rather obese, enough for two. One must never criticise these two because of their colour, for that would mean being antiarctic. Anyway, they claim that White isn't a colour at all.

One day Mummy Bear and Mummy Bear's non-binary sister, grumbling about the way the traditional roles still seemed to be being applied in this so-called progressive household, prepared some Whole-Grain Cereal with warm Bio-Soya Milk for breakfast. (My dear, 'porridge' is SO passé, not to mention stodgy and unhealthy.) They then went back upstairs to get dressed. While they were away, an asylum-seeking refugee child named Goldilocks, who despite her name was actually a brunette who had dyed her hair blonde and a part of it red and even had a bald patch at the rear, all in the name of Diversity, broke into the house through the rear door, slipped into the kitchen and helped herself to a couple of spoonsful of Whole-Grain Cereal with warm Bio-Soya Milk from each plate. Following which, belching slightly, she departed the kitchen as silently as she had come.

A few minutes later Daddy Bear, Daddy Bear's gay partner Teddy Bear, Mummy Bear, Mummy Bear's lover Fred Bear, Baby Bear, Baby Bear's bisexual Cousin and Polar Bear all came down for their eagerly-anticipated breakfast. (Not Bore as s/h/it was on a Diet, again, as s/h/it constantly and repetitively and obsessively explained, being worried about getting Bearlimia; Also Mummy Bear's non-Binary Sister had decided to lie down again for a while until she had worked out what this all meant in a Morning Cereal context, she was having one of her Adipose Episodes.) They were shocked at what they found. The MESS! Goldilocks had been in rather a hurry and had spilled a great deal of the Whole-Grain Cereal with warm Bio-Soya Milk.

"Who's been eating MY Whole-Grain Cereal with warm Bio-Soya Milk?" thundered Daddy Bear, feeling the aggression rising inside him and making a mental note to contact his Anger Counsellor later on.

"And Who's been eating MY Whole-Grain Cereal with warm Bio-Soya Milk?" asked Teddy Bear in what has to be admitted was a rather mincing tone, albeit he didn't eat mince, nor peppermince. "And WHO's been eating OUR Whole-Grain Cereal with warm Bio-Soya Milk??" screamed Mummy Bear on behalf of both herself and Fred, for it is time that the Females can speak also for the Males in modern society.

"Who's been eating My Whole-Grain Cereal with warm Bio-Soya Milk?" squealed Baby Bear, secretly relieved because he hated the stuff but Strawberry Jam, which he would have preferred, was not allowed because it meant cruelty to Strawberries and would be bad for his teeth.

Such dogmatists cannot bear an unanswered question. There has always to be Someone responsible for the ills of Society, whether these be the Capitalists or the Zionists or Both. Suspiciously they looked at each other. Had one of them come down earlier and ravaged their common breakfast? Who else could it be? So far as they knew (and they had spent many hours in dialectical debate on so many issues) there was neither a Capitalist nor a Zionist amongst them. Such a thought would be unbearable.

Mummy Bear came to what was left of her senses first. She went to the hallway next to the kitchen and opened the broom cupboard. Here sat Goldilocks, belching slightly and with definite traces of Soy Milk around her pouting lips.

"And who are YOU?" she asked, loudly and angrily.

"You mean, who are WE?" responded Goldilocks, tossing back her head. "We are a diverse set of personalities combined in one multi-coloured and non-gender-specific body. Be careful what you say to us or we shall accuse you of Sexism and Intolerance!"

"That sort of talk cuts no ice with Us here," responded Mummy Bear. "We are a licensed and authorised Diversity-Approved Ursine Household Collective, but YOU are an Outsider – not a member of an ethnic minority, nor a refugee from capitalist or colonialist or Zionist oppression, neither do you appear to be of the unemployed working class, nor a victim of sexist abuse whether physical or psychological. In short, and this is just a part of the list I am giving here, right, you look well dressed and well nourished and unscarred and so I wonder, what right do you think you have to come and eat OUR Breakfasts?"

Goldilocks was taken aback. She had not been expecting such a dogmatically and doctrinally-inclusive rejection of her legitimate claims. (ALL claims that people like her make are considered by those who make them to be legitimate.) She had to think quickly. "But I AM a refugee!" she wailed, "and I AM seeking asylum! Look, here is my identity card!"

Mummy Bear took it in her paw and inspected it carefully. "Well," she said thoughtfully, "then I suppose that changes everything. Just out of interest, from where are you a refugee, and why?"

Goldilocks had to think quickly again. The truth was that she was fleeing justice, having been caught by three bears in another cottage in another country stealing their porridge, but she had the feeling that this would not go down well right here, right now. So she said, "Well, there was this Big Bad Wolf, see, and he huffed and he puffed and he blew down half of my town, and so I and the others – whom I appear to have lost somewhere along the way – had to flee.

Oh, it was dreadful, first there was straw everywhere and then logs rolling all over the place and then the bricks... Oh..." She realised, too late, that her story with the bricks could not make sense and she could see from the glint in Mummy Bear's eye that she, too, was having difficulty in believing this tale.

"Sounds like a fairy story to me," she said. "So, you are fleeing a hairy mammal? One distantly related to us, as it happens? Can you prove this?"

Of necessity the story ends here. Political correctness would not allow any further description of subsequent events.

MORAL:- One needs Diversity in Adversity. This is a simple matter of Applied Bearology. But beware of Die-Versity.

****

No. 486 THE LITERARY DIET

Many a Writer likes to spread himself expansively out all over the page.

By employing multi-syllabic terminology of unnecessarily-excessive length and an overabundance of totally redundant hyphenated-syllables the impression may be given that the story is simply spreading out in an adipositive way all over the screen or the paper so as to leave hardly any space left unused.

One needs to take this verbosity in hand and apply some self-discipline. There is really no need for words that are so much longer than the context or the meaning requires. A little bit of blank paper and spaces can add character to a work. And so one day the Author decided to go onto a Diet.

It took great determination, but he did his best to cut out unnecessary intermediate paragraphs.

He left the descriptive passages to describe themselves more economically than he could.

He cut out dialogue and replaced it with monologue.

He used semi-colons more than colons;

Rather than flowery adjectives he used artificial minusjectives.

Deciding to go modern he omitted some quotation marks and other punctuation to save space

The narrative got thinner as more unnecessary and superfluous
adverbsly were discarded

The lines can be adequately reduced in their length
and still be perfectly adequate for fulfilling the job they have to do.
Not even judges like long sentences unless they are
really necessary.
Alternatives are sought
After some time and
effort the lines
are much shorter
and the page
less crowded.

It is true that
the narrative
is also a bit
thinner

...

The trouble is that as well
as managing to write more thinly there
is the problem of maintaining this thinness
once it has been attained. It is all too easy for the number
of words to start growing again as the pen sets
to work and the ink starts flowing and before you know it
you might have reached a rather weighty tome which then acquires
additional volumes and fills the entire bookcase again with their
weight adding pressure whilst their spines get dustier with lack of
use, so that one is back to where one had started before the diet and
feels even more of a failure.

MORAL:- Of course there is a range from light literature, serious and heavy literature to lite-rature. It has nothing to do with the weight of the paper, more the scope of the letterature employed.

****

No. 487   IMPORTANT STORY!

Dear Reader,

My name is Mumbo O'Gumbo M'Jumbo and I am an Attorney at Law in Suite F.A., Swindleton Towers, Fay Kadress, Lagos, Nigeria. I represent the late Mr. Suedo Nimm, a Writer who passed away in a dreadful road accident some years ago. He left a Literary Estate of 4 Million Words and left instructions for me to transfer this body of work to You.

I have now managed to trace you in accordance with his wishes and wish to effect the Transfer as soon as possible. Please send me the number of your Lending Library Card and a short story of your choice. Please open the attached Story and read it carefully. You will then receive fourteen volumes and enough to fill three metres of shelf space. Here is a sample to prove our authenticity.

"Once upon a Time there was a famous Swindler who sent people – unsuspecting individuals – messages that purported to be for their benefit. All they had to do was to reveal their private financial details, even PIN numbers and Pass Words would be asked for, and the intention was that the recipients would in this manner turn themselves unknowingly into victims and allow their literary bank accounts to be sucked dry on the nugatory promise of vast payments from an unknown deceased donor or publisher who had chosen them personally to be his beneficiary. Clearly enough people fell for this tale, and let themselves be duped, to make it worthwhile. They answered the unexpected message, believing that they would truly benefit from this kind offer from a Literary Agent of whom they had never heard, spinning a tale so bizarre (and so tragic in its details) that they felt themselves being spoken to directly..... and then found themselves opening books on their shelves that had turned totally blank, all the words had been syphoned off and were now being recycled in some foreign country, the words dismantled to allow individual letters to be put into different languages."

Please answer this message quickly in case we have to find some other Beneficiary. Write to me at the above address.

MORAL:- It is too late now for any Moral. By reading this far you have already kept this Story open for long enough......

****

No. 488   THE DOUBLE JIGSAW

People who do Jigsaw Puzzles for 'fun' are Masochists. This is obvious, for why else would they spend hours and hours laboriously putting together from small pieces of thin printed cardboard a picture that already exists on the cover of the box, and then, once it is finished at last, pull it apart again afterwards? Large portions of their lives are wasted in this way. But the TRUE Masochists go even further.

It is only in <u>very</u> specialist shops that you will find the Double Jigsaws. These come in different forms. Caution – you need to be strong to read further.

The simplest and perhaps the beginning of the craze was when Poddingtons brought out the 'Jigsaw Squared' series for Xmas in – when was it now? A few years ago now and, to the best of my knowledge, very few have ever been completed. This is not in fact 'squared' but simply 'doubled', though I doubt if any mathematician would complain. It comprises TWO sets of jigsaw pieces in ONE box! The true aficionados, who do after all have a lot of time to spare in their asylums, will pour all these out onto a large table and then try to do both jigsaws at the same time, without looking at the box!! Of course, with the two sets of pieces there are eight corners, eight sides with straight edges, and two very different sets of colourful pictures. One picture is on the lid of the box, the other will be printed on an insert (but Upside Down!!)

Then you have the TWO-SIDED Jigsaws – which, as their name explains, are printed on each side so that the final picture can be either the A side or the B side.... but there is no way of telling which side is which until you have fitted all the pieces together! Again, there will be two pictures to copy as a guide, one on the lid and one on the base of the lid, so that you cannot look at both at the same time but need to keep turning the lid over and over. This is guaranteed to cause hours of merry fun in the family, or at least in the Family Court.

Now there are two types of these as well. For the absolute masochists you have both sides of the pieces printed with the same picture! This does not of course mean that each piece is the same on both sides, oh no! - for its shape and its exact content will depend where it should be placed in relation to all the other pieces. But should one ever manage to complete the jigsaw then there will be exactly the same picture facing the table as facing upwards. And for the professionals, these are sold in PLAIN boxes.

There are confused reports from the last Jigsaw Association Festival which was held in Clacton from October to November. (Most of these festivals are held in resorts during periods when there is nothing better to do outdoors and accommodation is cheaper – the custom began with Weston-super-Mare, spreading to Morecambe and later Bridlington for the Northern League.) At these traditional Festivals up to twenty opposing teams of up to three persons are allocated at random a large regulation flat table and a 5,000-piece Jigsaw in a sealed box to complete against the clock. Although personal needs breaks are permitted and players are encouraged to get at least two hours sleep in every forty-eight, with medical staff on duty in case of necessity, it has been known for teams to work on non-stop even after all other teams have completed their assignments – they simply cannot stop with the work left unfinished. Very occasionally there are rumours of sabotage, with teams removing a single piece from their competitors' table......

However, with this Clacton 'Double-Vision' themed festival devoted to the Double-Sided Jigsaws it seems violence broke out after about the fifth hour and some very unsporting behaviour was displayed, with tables overturned, pieces scattered and both judges were eventually forced to flee the site leaving the competition unfinished. The Police were eventually called in following charges of Disturbing the Pieces. Voices have been heard that these are really a Piece too Far and that from now on such Double-Sided works should be available only in enclosed medical institutions where there is no time pressure and no sense of competitiveness to make matters more difficult.

It remains to be seen what effect these events will have on the normal domestic tradition of giving each other brightly-coloured jigsaws of landscapes, bookshelves, portrait galleries, cloudscapes and other forms of mental torture to ensure that family holidays will descend into competitive and obsessive conflict. Family Xmases will for decades to come be punctuated by cries of "I think this fits! Look! Oh no, it doesn't, not quite, what about this one?"

MORAL:- If the piece doesn't fit, maybe YOU should have a fit instead? That would be a fitting end.

****

No. 489 REGULATIONS

I'm sorry Sir, Madam, but you cannot read this Story until I have checked your authorisation. Sorry Sir, but being the Author does not by itself include authorisation. It would be more than my job's worth if I let you go on without checking first. Why, there's no knowing what might happen if you get reading further, Sir.

First, Sir, can you prove you are over Fifteen Years of Age? I mean Reading Age, actually. This story is marked for Adults, you can see that, it's not one of your kiddy airy-fairy stories with happy endings, you know, it could be mentally disturbing for a young reader who's not properly prepared and adequately escorted. Yes Sir, please don't get upset, I'm just following the Regulations, Sir, I can see you have a grey beard, but kids these days, Sir, you won't believe what they get up, anything to see inside an Adult Novel – wigs, hair dyes, you name it. No stopping the little blighters sometimes. But it's more than me job's worth - here at the Literary Inspectorate. Sir, I can't help you if you want to spit – that's the Expectorate you'll need then, Sir. Can't do anything for you about that – it's more than me job's worth.

What makes it an Adult Novel? Well Sir, that's not for me to say Sir, it's in the Regulations. Maybe it's to do with what goes on between the covers, ha ha, just my little joke, Sir. Used that one many a time.

Do you have a Certificate of Education? O-Level, A-Level, S-Level? Or one of those foreign Baccy things? Something to prove you have read Books before and are qualified for more? No Sir, a Library Ticket isn't enough anymore these days, they are too easily forged. We need to see an original document, or, well, it's more than me job's worth. Ah, so you say you have a Doctorate? Do you have any proof on you, Sir, apart from your visiting card with the title? I mean, Anyone could get cards printed, couldn't they? Easy as anything these days, it is. No-one checks, it's appalling, if you ask me. No respect for titles.

And then you get people who just want to copy ideas, take them over, pass them off as their own. There's a big market in that sort of thing these days, Sir. Just imagine, someone could prove it was done by someone who'd read a book that I was in charge of? Gives me the shivers, that does. More than me job's worth, that is.

Well, look, Sir, seeing as how it's you and all that – and you say you wrote it yourself anyway - I <u>Could</u> just let you read on a bit, to the end of the next paragraph or two, all right? But please, do promise me, you won't tell anybody? It's more than me job's worth, really.

Me? Oh, I CAN read, of course I can, learned it ages ago, but, well, I don't read much myself, you know, not anymore, but that's probably better that way – it would be more than my job's worth if I was to look through all the things we get sent to check over, I can tell you.

<u>MORAL</u>:- If you ask me, some Jobs are not worth having anyway.

****

No. 490   THE PIGGY BANK

There was once a Piggy Bank. It was owned by a piggy banker, who was himself a bit of a swine. He consumed whatever he could find, even odd scraps, and produced only shit. He was thick-skinned and bristly and had eyes too small for his head. Despite this, people said he was very intelligent. "Give me all your itty-bitty coins!" he would tell the children, "'And I shall keep them safe in my belly for as long as I can and then eventually return them to you, with no interest whatsoever! If in the meantime you want access to any of your funds or even a loan, I shall tell you that it is impossible to open me yet without endangering the entire financial system."

Being involved in the fine finesses of the finance world, he often told porkies and was not above hamming it up. "I am here to save MY bacon, not yours!" he would say if challenged. "The only futures which count, as far as I am concerned, are Pork Futures. Mine."

"Swine, swimmin' and song" were his main interests. Pigs are mammals not fowl and therefore the nest eggs of their investors are none of their concerns. However stylish the sty, it remains true that bankers prefer much feeding at the trough and swinish slumber to actual concern for the financial health of their clients. "'Snout to do with me," he'd say. "There's Free Swill and they must make their own decisions. I've seen clients make some rasher investments in my time. Up for the chop, they were. But don't blame me." He would bristle. "Always look on the silver back," he warned and squealed loudly. He was quite a boar but he claimed to make Sownd investments even when the steaks were high.

He began to speculate in property and acquired houses built of straw, of wood and of brick from his poorer brethren, but although considered respectable, this is a form of gammonbling and there are always risks that prices may fall as much as the houses when a cold

205

wind blows...... Eventually he learned that his own bankers were likelier to foreclose upon a mortgage than close upon a greengage and that few creatures are sorrier for themselves than a pig in a poke.

MORAL:- 'OneSty is the best policy.

****

No. 491   THE OBSESSIVE

There was once a man who, not to put too fine a point upon it, in fact, essentially and inseparably from the rest of his character, all other things being considered, tended towards, well, a feeling of, if one may so express it, Obsession. Little things that most people just ignore would play a large part in his daily thinking. He would notice things that others would not notice – a speck of dust, a picture not QUITE straight, a smear, and to make matters worse he had this constant need – it was not a desire, it was a real NEED – constantly to go back and check on things - for he had this constant insecurity. On leaving his home to go to work he would get halfway down the path and then pause, deep in sudden worry. Had he turned the lights off? Had he unplugged the kettle? Had he watered the plants sufficiently? Had he closed the door properly? Had he locked it? Had he double-locked it? HAD HE REMEMBERED TO TAKE HIS KEYS? Fiddling in his coat pocket would resolve the last of these worries but then there was nothing for it but to turn back, unlock the door, check all the things AGAIN (because of course he had already checked them at least once before leaving) and then – then closing the door and...

I'd better just pause here and go back over that first paragraph again. Did I get the spellings all correct? Was that opening sentence not too, well, banal? Does it grip properly? Let's just give it a quick read-through and a check over and... well, it seems all right, I suppose, not one of my best, but, well, it'll do for now.

By this time of course he would be getting a bit late for his train, the 08.13 from the local station. A quick pat of his pockets. Had he got his Season Ticket? Watch? Briefcase? Any files he had brought home from work to deal with at home in the evening? At this point he would have to flick open his brief case and peek inside, flick through the papers, satisfy himself that all was rightly present, straighten them up again, close his case again and continue towards the station but oh my goodness it was already 08.11 by now... better walk really quickly now and not stop again....

Did I write it was the <u>08.13</u> train? I'm not quite sure about that now, come to think of it, maybe I ought to check with a timetable? I think the next one, if he missed the 08.13, was only at 08.22 which isn't too bad a wait in the circumstances but even so would mean getting a later bus from the destination station and getting to the office at the last minute at 08.59 rather than a more comfortable 08.45.

Now at last he was on the platform. People were still waiting there, regulars, so he knew he had not yet missed the 08.13 which, indeed, was approaching right now! Would it have four carriages or six? He normally sat in the fourth, which was either the end one or somewhere in the middle. But he liked to note the numbers down so if it was, say, a four-car and a two-car set coupled together then he would want to note down both numbers which meant standing a bit to the right so as to see the number on the second set too. Later he would write these numbers into his Diary.

It is dreadful, having an insecure memory. In fact, allow me a minute and I'll just read through what I have written so far, just in case. One can never be too sure. Punctuation, missing spaces between words, that sort of thing. I might even have repeated something.

You know, I am really not sure if this story is ready yet for finishing. Let me just proof read it one more time and get some checking done...

MORAL:- There is no need to get obsessive about being obsessive.... though it's better than being obese.

****

No. 492   THE PREQUEL

Before a Story can properly begin there is a lot that has to be done in preparation. These things do not, in spite of the impression they like to make, just "happen by themselves". Let us take as an example a classic form of Fairy Tale in which a Princess lives in a Castle and yearns to meet the Prince of her dreams, and so on. There are many versions of this basic theme, but they all tend to start the same way. (They nearly all end with a vague "Happy Ever After" without ever defining what that actually means; Pension and savings schemes use the same selling technique.)

But - before this you have to construct the Castle with all its towers, moats, drawbridges, pennants that fly, deep dungeons and more. The land has to be bought or conquered, architects engaged, stone quarried and transported, wooden scaffoldings erected – it's a big job, building a Castle and getting it ready before even the Contents Page. The King and Queen have to meet, fall in love, marry and (ahem) cause the Princess to be born – these things, dear children, DO NOT just happen by themselves! I have a feeling that storks and cabbages, but not cabbage stalks are involved. Palace Guards need to be recruited, uniformed, provided with weapons, trained and set in their positions. Chancellors need time to grow old and (hopefully) wise with long beards and of course the same applies to witches. As with a film, you need experts to handle the costumes and the casting and the location scouts and the construction of sets and the choice of landscapes and a thousand-and-one other things, not counting the issues of Rights to certain sub-plots and Financing and Insurance (what if the wrong actress were to prick her thumb? What if one of the Dragons were to get out of control and roast, then eat his handler?) Popular Princesses get many offers to appear in several Stories at once so one needs special Multi-Story car parks for their vehicles – a limousine here, a horse and carriage there, a Royal State Carriage for another.... A glass carriage with slipper brakes....

The Princes (there are usually several of them even though only one is destined to succeed – a bit like semen in a symbolic sort of way –

hence the phrase 'some day my Prince will come') need to be raised, taught to ride horses gallantly, wave spears dangerously, lean back and smile casually.... and accept failure graciously. If animals are involved (usually small mammals, often rodents but also deer, foxes, dogs, cats, wolves, wise owls and the like) then they need Language Coaches and the chance to learn their script at a pace to suit themselves. This takes time; Many a film director has had a close squeak when working with animals.

Sometimes gardeners and foresters are required to create clearings in woods and small romantic but shabby huts with crooked chimncys. Contact needs to be made with the Magicians', Wizards and Witches Union (MWWU) and terms agreed also for the many minor characters who will form the admiring crowds but only appear in one paragraph or on one page (including the page boys). Prrof reading (see what I mean?), editing, printing and binding have to be organised, the quality of paper, the type of illustrations....

And THEN at last, when everything has been checked and double-checked (one wants no loose ends in a story!) one can start the Reading! Are we all ready now? Very well. Then we'll begin:

"Once upon a Time......"

MORAL:- One should <u>never</u> begin at the Beginning. There is always so much to do first....

****

No. 493   DOES READING CAUSE CANCER?

Great interest and alarm was raised last month, when a report in an obscure medical Journal revealed that of the 1,274 adult patients who in the past twelve months had died of various forms of cancer in a specific sample, all of them had been to school, acquired literacy in childhood and read books. The link seemed just too obvious to deny and (following some hysterical television reports) led to an immediate drop in the purchase of books both from bookshops (three closed within two weeks) and online.

Of course, one of the main activities of modern science is to find ways each month to cause alarm and despondency in the population, thus leading to an increase in deaths through high blood pressure, heart attacks or depression due to reading bad news. There is nothing new about this; Two hundred years ago a major health concern was equine manure and urine in the streets; then later came concerns about soot and smog from steam locomotives and mills burning coal; This was followed by concerns regarding breathing invisible particles of sulphur dioxide produced by Diesel engines; To this can now be added worries connected with the use of Electricity - for those living near wind generators, to those living close to masts where high-frequency signals are sent out for mobile phone networks, or those living close to high-voltage transmission cables and pylons, or current concerns whether the drivers of electric cars will be electrocuted during storms. We can assume this trend will continue; It is, after all, not so long ago that the presence of Bubonic Plague, Smallpox or Typhoid was linked to the presence of ethnic or religious minorities who apparently and allegedly had nothing better to do than to poison the communal water supply.

But - This month's issue of the same Journal (the 'Journal for Alarmist Medicine') has led to a relaxation from this state of literary panic. Or at least, it should have done. Several responses were published disagreeing with the thesis of the article last month. It appears that in developing countries where the majority of the adult population suffer from varying degrees of chronic Analphabetism, whether or not combined with a profound cranial ignorance, there is still a mortality rate of 100%. So maybe Reading alone is not the main cause of Morbidity.

In this case one factor contributing to the alarm has turned out to be the use of automatic "spellcheckers" which automatically completed or altered words to suit the computer's electronic dictionary. Neither the authors of the paper nor the editors of the Journal nor the proof-readers nor the so-called 'peer reviewers' seemed to have noticed this. So 'tumour' should have read 'humour' throughout. The word 'can' was often automatically extended to 'cancer' and 'cancel' likewise. It seems to have been a false alarm all along.

The only trouble is – apart from me, and I HAD to read it as part of my job at the publishers', I don't think anyone else I know has yet picked up the nerve to read the responses!

MORAL:- if you have got this far, then you may as well relax. Either there is no problem, or it is too late anyway.

****

No. 494   HORRORSCOPE

Astrology is the name for one form of the study of the Stars. No, not like Astronomers who wish to measure distances and the power and distribution of light sources, galactic dust clouds, black holes, quasars and other phenomena; nor in the form of tabloid journalists for whom anyone who has ever had a minor part in a single episode of some soap opera – a mere transient bubble in the Soap – is a 'Star' whose every activity needs to be minutely documented and publicised; Instead they study those heavenly bodies (I forbear to draw any comparison with "Starlets" whose main claim to notice is the same thing) which, it is considered, exert an influence over an insignificant small blue-green spinning planet in a solar system billions of light years away. No-one has ever explained WHY an invisible incalculable force billions of light-years away should have any influence upon the Earth or individual or collective human destinies, but Theologians are wary of saying so too loudly, in case Astrologers make the same accusations back at them. Neither has anyone researched yet whether this quasi-gravitational system works both ways, whether the Earth has any influence on, say, the emotions or destinies of any inhabitants of Venus or Mercury.

Still, a remarkable number of newspapers still publish somewhere in the back pages, under the weather forecasts, shares advice and the racing tips, where the most gullible optimists always look, daily forecasts of what the immediate future may bring to those of its readers who can still read and care; These on the basis merely of their dates of birth which neatly and irrevocably allocate them into specific categories – the category including February of course always having fewer, but no-one seems to mind. (The newspapers cater to the gullible pessimists on other pages dedicated to political analyses instead.) There are considered to be three each of the Water, Air, Earth and Fire signs – combined into two pairs, which make respectively Liquid Mud and Hot Air. Here are some typical examples:

AQUARIUS. The Water Carrier

January 20 – February 18.

Beware of Water. People drown in it. Stick to Beer, make sure the taps are turned off, and don't kick the Bucket.

PISCES. The Fish

February 19 – March 20.

Today is a good day for reading your Horoscope, as it will be otherwise a fairly empty, boring period. Some fishy plots may be encountered. Eat plenty of chips and peas.

ARIES. The Ram

March 21 – April 19.

Be careful of rampant thoughts and plots getting out of control. Your thoughts might turn to sheep. Eat mutton.

TAURUS. The Bull.

April 20 – May 20.

You may find yourself today on the horns of a dilemma. Beware of Bullshit and avoid the colour red and men in fancy costumes who try to bully you.

GEMINI. The Twins

May 21 – June 20.

There could be some duplication in your narrative; Get a lector to check over it properly. There could be some duplication in your narrative; Get a lector to check it over properly. Note: NOT Hannibal Lector and not a Collector.

CANCER. The Crab

June 21 – July 22.

Do not get caught in the pincers of time. Now is not a good time to come out of your shell.

LEO. The Lion

July 23 – August 22nd.

A good day for lying around with a good book. This is the mane thing. One has to mane-tain one's Pride.

VIRGO. The Virgin

August 23rd.- September 22nd.

It would be best for you to stay tucked up alone in bed with a good book; that way you may be able to stay the way you are.

LIBRA. The Scales

September 23rd. - October 22nd.

Maybe you should scale back on your reading, or balance it with other Interests.

SCORPIO. The Scorpion

October 23rd. - November 21st.

Try to stick with crime thrillers or spy stories; these usually have a sting in the tail.

SAGITTARIUS. The Archer

November 22nd. - December 21st.

Set yourself a target of three hours of reading per day. Avoid the bull's eye or Tauri may get upset at you.

CAPRICORN. The Goat

Dec. 22nd – January 19th.

Stop kidding yourself; Billy and Nanny cannot look after you for ever. It is time for you to learn to read something other than Horoscopes. Otherwise a poor future can be safely predicted for you and you will never become a furry overgoat.

MORAL:- For those who believe in the power of distant heavenly bodies, there is no need for Morals since everything is already foreseen, billions of years ago. It is just a matter of waiting until the ineffable cosmic influence hits our spinning globe.

****

No. 495   A SSSSERPENTINE WHINE

A Sssssnake hisssssssssssed to itself. It wanted dessssssperately to find itsssssself a mate and do ssssssssome kisssssssing and of courssssssssse it issssssss not eassssssy to hisssssss and kisssssssss at the sssssssssame time. Not only that, if two ssssssnakessss ssssssstart doing tonguessssssss, there isssssss a ssssstrong rissssssssk that at leasssssssssst one of them will get poisssssssssssoned. Very frusssssssstrating.

What issss the point of looking phallic and being sssssso flexssssssible if one'sssss ssexssss life isssss so dull? What issss the point of being able to sssshed a ssssssskin just like that, to wriggle out of it and get ssssssstark ssssnaking naked, if the other keepssssss her ssssscalessssss on?

On a hot rock he ssssspied a lady ssssnake – at leasssssst, from a dississtancssse it looked like one; maybe he would at lasssssst ssssstrike lucky? Ssssssslowly he sssslithered towardssssss her. But how to sssssstart? He had no exsssssperiencssse.

Ssssssssnakes are divided into two typessss; Ssshould they Ssssssswallow or Sssssqueeeeze? The contradictionssss of Consssstrictionsssss allow one to put the ssssssqueeze on ssssssomeone when the money issss tight. One has coilssss and spiralsssss. It isss not the female'ssss tassssssk to wear the Coil.

"Hi there Ssssssweeetie," he said, waving hisssss head in a ssssssinuoussss but not necssesssssarily ssssssinful fashion – more ssssssenssssuoussssly, he hoped. "I usssssed to be in filmssssss. Cobra Five-Oh, that wassssss one of mine! Like my hood? Hey, you look like you could be an adder! Wanna add sssssomething to me? Got any grasssss-ssssssnake?"

"Who do you think you are?'" she replied. "An anaconda? A python? Jusssst look at your grubby sssssnakesssssskin outfit."

"Hey, I can't help it!" he sssaid. "It'ssss in the Bible, like, how we all gotta go in the dusssssst. Hey, give me a ssssign! Or even....." (he paused) "a Cosssssine would be better!"

"My bite is worssssse than your bark," she ssssaid, trying to outsssssssstare him..

"Hey, don't get rattled!" he ssssaid. "Unlesss, of coursssse, you're a Rattlesssssnake!"

She looked at him with dissssgussssst. "You're Hisssstory," she sssaid.

The ssssnake sssslinked off to find sssssome fore-prey (or even a mousssse as paw-prey) to offer asssss a gift, but hissss heart jussssssst wassssn't in it anymore. A Ssssssnake-Charmer, he wasssssn't.

MORAL:- Ssssometimesss you sshould jusssssst pisssss off! And be careful when picking up a vindsscreen viper.

****

No. 496   THE JOGGER

There was once a man who decided to go Jogging. He had been told by well-meaning friends that it would do him good. So he bought some tight sporty shiny shorts ("Marathongs") and some hefty lace-up running shoes and a singlet and he already had a Walkman and so getting up one morning he put on the tight shorts and the singlet and the socks and the running shoes and he inserted the earpieces from his Walkman into his ears and he unlocked his door and he went out and he locked his door and put the keys in his tight trouser pocket and went onto the pavement and turned left and he jogged and jogged and jogged and jogged and jogged and jogged and jogged and jogged and jogged and jogged and jogged and jogged and jogged and jogged and jogged and jogged and jogged and jogged and jogged but then he came to some traffic lights at Red so he STOPped and stood there breathing deeply in and out and in and out and bent down to rub his knees but then the lights changed again so he braced himself upright once more and jogged until he came to the Park where he turned in through the Main Gate and then jogged and jogged and jogged and jogged and jogged and jogged and jogged and jogged and jogged and jogged along the broad main driveway then turned right to go past the Lake and through the bushes and round the back and out at the Rear Entrance and then back onto the road where he jogged and jogged and jogged and jogged and jogged and jogged and jogged and jogged and jogged and jogged, quite sweaty by now but still listening to the music on his earphones, which meant that when he came to the next road he jogged and jogged and jogged and jogged and jogged and jogged and jogged and jogged and jogged and jogged and didn't see the lorry coming but luckily it JUST missed him, hooting loudly and angrily, so he paused a bit to get his breath back and then turned up the hill and jogged and jogged and jogged and jogged and jogged until he was half-way up and then he dropped Dead.

Just like that.

It was a bit of a shock and of course he had no identification on him in his tight shiny sports trousers so it took a little while to work out which door the keys in his pocket would match, but eventually his affairs were sorted out and a funeral was arranged and I do believe he jogged all the way to Heaven, though he was not let in until he had got himself more decently clothed.

MORAL:- Sometimes to be a tight fit in your trousers is better than to have a tight fit in your trousers.

****

No. 497   PACKAGING

My Beloved wanted to give me a Story as a present and came with an

ENORMO
US
PACKAGE

You can imagine how I felt!!! First I had to open the BOX which was TIED WITH STRING that I had to cut HERE and HERE as the Knots were too tight. I opened the lid. Inside was a lot of extruded fibreglass thingummies and a

PARCEL WRAPPED IN
PRETTY
DECORATIVE PAPER

This was sealed with sticky tape, so first I tried carefully to slide it open without tearing the paper, but this didn't work, so eventually it all got rather torn in any case. But it was already very exciting.

Having cleared away the Wrapping Paper I found inside a thin CARDBOARD BOX with some pictures on the outside and the name of the Manufacturer (or 'Author' as they are known in this case.) One of my Favourites! Eagerly I turned the BOX this way and that to see how best to open it. It turned out that the top was simply a lid which, when you held it carefully, slip upwards and off the lower, inner section. Hurrah!

Inside the BOX there was some PLASTIC BUBBLE WRAP SHEET which was wrapped around another packet. With increasing excitement, almost a frenzy, I unwrapped the BUBBLE WRAP and found inside a large JIFFY BAG with my name written on it!

The JIFFY BAG was sealed at the end with the two sides of the flap firmly fixed to each other. I pulled it open with some force, to find a small PACKET inside.

Inside the little PACKET was a piece of PAPER, folded up. I opened it and there was a STORY. It began:

Once upon a
time there was
a Story that
was very
fragile and
needed to be
well wrapped
up against all
sorts of outside
influences......

MORAL:- Sometimes the secret lies in the Packaging.

No. 498   PACKAGING INFORMATION

LITERADON ANTI-BOREDOM MEDICATION. 20 microplots.

READ THE INSTRUCTIONS

This patented STORY is wrapped for Extra Freshness: The Wrapping is recyclable; as is the Story itself. The Plot, Descriptions, Characters can all be re-used in appropriate formats.

DOSEAGE: 2 Pages three times a day. Read Between and not During Meals. Do not Over-read. Always follow instructions on the labels or chapter headings.

Observe Page Numbers carefully. Do not turn more than One Page at a time as this can lead to excessive Pagination. Read One Page at a time and do not repeat unless necessary.

CAUTION: Contains Raw Fiction. Do not read after advised Time. (See Below). Can affect Sleep Patterns and Dreams.

READ BEFORE: 21.00.

NOT FOR CHILDREN aged 15 and Under. Can cause Nightmares.

SIDE EFFECTS: For possible Side Effects see the Footnotes inside the packaging.

Side Effects can include:

- An enhanced Fantasy.

- Internal Visions.
- Hearing Voices inside one's head while reading Dialogue.
- Increased tension when approaching Climaxes.
- Sleeplessness and Inability to Close Book.
- Sense of Frustration when the Story is completed.
- Desire to read Sequels.
- Enhanced Desire to Discuss the Narrative.
- Memories.

CAUTION: Reading could lead to Headaches, Eyestrain, Overheated Fantasies and subsequent Guilt Feelings. If in doubt consult your nearest Librarian.

IN EMERGENCY: In case of Overreading: Turn off Light and Close Eyes.

MORAL:- Reading is a Drug. Do not get addicted!

****

No. 499   THE MOBILE

There is a growing feeling that the endless use of mobile phones is destroying social intercourse. Just look at any group of people in a train, in a café, on a bench, and you will see that, rather than communicating with each other, talking, playing, joking, singing or anything else, the half of them at least are staring at their little screens and tapping with a finger or thumb on the on-screen keyboard.

It seems we have this desperate need to be always accessible, always on call, always available for anyone – *Dingalingalongdong* oh, sorry, let me take this... Hello, yes, Oh, hi, look, I'm sorry, I'm with someone right now, can I call you back? Yes? OK, promise, alright? Bye!

     o   yes, for anyone to get hold of us at any moment, day or night.

Dingalingalongdong Hello, hello? Yes? I cannot hear... Oh, it's You! Look I'm sorry but I cannot talk right now darling, all right? I'll get back to you soonest, promise promise, byeeeeee! - Yes, to be always accessible means that one lives one's life in a totally different way, never knowing when the next interrup- *Dingalingalongdong* - No, I can't right now, it's not a good time, I'm just in the middle of explaining something to the readers, can you call back this evening? Thanks. - So anyone can call at any time about any subject, even things that *Dingalingalongdong* Hello? No, no thanks, I don't want a new super economy tariff, thanks, I'll stick with the one I have. - And then there are all these Apps that can distract you, I don't just mean the useful ones with a map or a timetable but really, who needs to know how many Indian restaurants there are within two kilometres? Or the weather in Melbourne? Even if I were going there, it would have changed by the time I got there. But there are these endless lists of things you can download and you see kids these days *Dingalingalongdong* Hello? Oh, thanks, yes, that sounds nice, but I am not sure if I can manage the 3rd.... I am busy right now, can't get to my diary, can I call you back later and confirm that? Thanks, Bye! - so, to get back to what I was saying, I am sure that it can be a great benefit to have the ability to stay in touch with people wherever you are, but at the same time, I – ***Dingalingalongdong*** Hello, yes, er, No, I'm sorry, I don't know where she is, shall I tell her you called if I see her? Yes, gladly, anything urgent? No, all right, I see, well, thanks and, yes, I'll do that, 'bye. That was your husband, dear, oh, I'm SO sorry, Darling, I have been a bit distracted, you know how it is – did you have your orgasm yet?

MORAL:- It takes more than a Smartphone to make you smart.

. . . .

****

No. 500   MERETRICIOUS METRICATION AND HOW TO READ THE METER

Here is a Letter:

A. (This is actually a Milliletter.)

Here are: Ten Letters. (= A Deciletter)

Ten letters squared; If this were to be multiplied by itself, thus making Ten times Ten letters, it would make a total of exactly =

a Hundred Letters. (A Centiletter)

It is also possible to employ a large number of Letters in a se (50) quence of sentences and almost fill an entire paragraph wit (100) h them. Even though we do not count the spaces between them, nor (150) the various punctuation marks such as commas or semi-colons and hyphens, but just the (200) normative letters themselves, and avoid inserting any digi (250) ts, the constituents of the Alphabet, so to speak,

With a little effort one can reach the next decimal total - a Thousand letters! (= A Kiloletter) But too many of these would make heavy reading.

MORAL: Be grateful you aren't paying per letter.

****

About the Author

Rabbi Dr. Walter Rothschild is a writer, broadcaster and cabaret artist who has worked as a community rabbi in the UK, Aruba, Germany, Poland and Austria.   He is a railway historian and an expert on railways and the Holocaust and also railways of the Middle East.
 Further information about him can be found on:

www.walterrothschild.de

www.rabbiwalterrothschild.de

www.rothschild-comedy.de

www.harakevet.com

(Some of the) other books by the author:

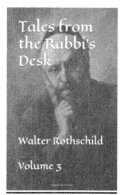

SHERLOCK HOLMES' BOOKCASE

Volumes 1 & 2.

The term 'Sherlock Holmes' has come to indicate an ascetic, meticulous observer, one whose deductive powers were useful for the detection of many a criminal and the resolution of many a literary mystery. But surely there was another side to the man, and also to his faithful companion and 'Boswell', Dr. John Watson? What sort of men were they, what were their backgrounds, what were their concerns? Over the years many have tried - with varying degrees of failure - to emulate Arthur Conan-Doyle's original writings; there are even some humourless obsessives who will criticise every comma they deem misplaced. Nevertheless, we now present a new collection of stories, discovered by accident, possibly even written by accident, and designed to be read by accident. Rather than the detective's Casebook, this is more a Bookcase, mixed volumes standing side by side and on those vague borders between fiction and fantasy. The reader may explore further at their own risk.

TALES OF THE CHUTZPER REBBE

Lost in the mists, swamps and forests of Eastern Europe, plagued by mosquitoes and Cossacks (though not necessarily in that order) lies the almost-forgotten *Shtetl* of Chutzp. Here is the seat of one of the lesser-known Hasidic dynasties - The Chutzper Hasidim, that mystic, anti-intellectual, ecstatic sect that placed so much emphasis on a close encounter with *Hashem*, facilitated when necessary through a haze of schnapps. With a tinge of nostalgia we look back at some of the founders of this Hasidic school, their disciples and others whose lives were touched by their unique view of this world and the next.

THERE'S TROUBLE DOWN AT T'PITCH!

Football as it really was.   Memories of Huddersfax City and Cleckheckmondsedge Rovers in the glory days. As told by a Father to his Son. Football in Yorkshire, back in the 1920's to the 1950's – How was it really? These affectionate tales of the glory days of Cleckheckmondsedge Rovers and Huddersfax City won't exactly give the answer to this question, but hopefully they will enlighten and entertain – and may even explain a little of what went on inside the heads under those cloth caps huddled under the rainclouds in the old pictures in the papers.

CRYPTIC TALES FROM THE CRYPT

Memoirs of an Undertaker's Undertakings
Or: My Apprenticeship with Death.

By Henry A. H. Longbottom - As told to Dr. Walter Rothschild.

Mr. Henry Longbottom spent some years in his youth as an Apprentice at Thistlethwaites' Funeral Directors and we are fortunate to have some recorded interviews in which he recalls some of the events of that period. Apart from keeping the premises tidy - it is the Apprentice who usually has to Brush with Death - he had to accompany the senior staff on many jobs and picked up many a fascinating tale from those who had worked there longer. These 'Cryptic Tales' are now presented by the Shadley Local History Society, edited by its Chairman Dr. Walter Rothschild.

AESOP'S FOIBLES VOLUMES 1 - 6 (and beyond

Aesop's Fables have been famous for over two and a half millennia; Aesop's Foibles have only been around for a rather shorter time, but one lives in hope. Providing a different and usually unexpected perspective on a variety of everyday situations and combinations, they challenge the reader in many ways to retain their composure, stability and indeed sanity while observing life from a different angle. Nothing is impossible in an allegorical universe, from jokes that work to similes that smile, bodily functions that function and metaphors that are actually taken from a parallellellell dididimension. The good news is: Each Volume is Finite.

TALES FROM THE RABI'S DESK - VOLUMES 1 - 4
And Beyond

As a Rabbi I had been taught always to look behind a story, to see what is hiding in the spaces between the letters and between the lines...... to be aware of other dimensions; To be sensitive, like Elijah the prophet, to still, small voices." Rabbi Dr. Walter Rothschild brings us a collection of stories, some fictional and many based on factual experiences, based on several decades of work as a congregational Rabbi in England and in Europe.

These stories give an insight into the rich tapestry of human lives that he and his colleagues have touched.

Printed in Great Britain
by Amazon

79635109R00132